C000079969

WHAT READERS ARE SAYING...

ABOUT MAGGIE AWARD OF EXCELLENCE
FINALIST, *ENSNARED BY INNOCENCE*:

"Witty, Enchanting and Roaring Hot!
I think I've found a new author to binge! I
would definitely recommend it as a good gateway
book to shape-shifters or to lovers of historical
romance."
5-Star Goodreads Review

"I would give this a 10/10 rating. **Beautifully
written by a very talented author... PLEASE
read this brilliant novel.** I cannot wait for the
next in series."
5-Star BookBub Review

"Oh. My. Goodness! This story caught my
attention from page one. It is a fresh take on the

shifter genre. **This Regency novel had every element a girl could want: several mysteries to solve, smokin' hot heroes and sensible, funny and courageous heroines.**"
5-star Goodreads review

"**Without a doubt, this author is going to the top of my favorite historical novel author list. I really loved this twist on the traditional historical romance novel.**"
5-star Goodreads review

"**Fantastic Story!!** I really enjoyed this book!" 5-Star Reviewer Emily P.

"I love the fact this is **shifter and regency** all rolled into one...I was amazed by the storyline and couldn't help how addictive I found this text...**I loved the originality of this book** and thought it really stood out for many reasons... **A true talent for writing...**"
5-Star Review

Rescued by a Christmas Kiss © 2023 Larissa Lyons.
Published by Literary Madness.

No AI contributed to this story; 100% human effort.

ISBN
978-1-949426-99-1 E-book
978-0-9834711-8-9 Print
978-1-949426-65-6 Large Print

Don't be a scurvy pirate! (Save that for Thorne.) Only read
legitimately purchased books.

All rights reserved, including the right to decide how to
market this book. By law, no part of this publication may be
copied, uploaded or transferred without written permission.

Please respect the hard work of this author and only read
authorized, purchased downloads. All characters are fictional
creations; any resemblance to actual persons is unintentional
and coincidental.

Cover by Literary Madness. Proofread by Judy Zweifel at
Judy's Proofreading.

At Literary Madness, our goal is to create a book free of typos.

If you notice anything amiss, please let us know. litmadness@
yahoo.com

NO Generative or other AI uses Permitted.

Author and Publisher reserve all rights to this content, both
text and cover. No person or entity may reproduce and/or
otherwise use this content in any manner, including for
purposes of training artificial intelligence technologies. With
the exception of brief quotes in reviews (one to two sentences
in length) no other use may be made of this content without
the Author and Publisher's specific, express, and written
permission.

CONTENTS

CONTENTS

RESCUED BY A CHRISTMAS KISS

A WARM AND WITTY WINTER REGENCY

LARISSA LYONS

But she...was in a moment as much overcome by her happiness as she had been before by her fears.

— JANE AUSTEN, *SENSE AND SENSIBILITY*

>

1

CRASH!

London

A FAST-MOVING blur caught his attention.

Barnabas left off his task and gazed out the window, past the frost and steam from his gentle *huff*. The stranger scuttled across the rain-slicked street, heading his way.

More disarrayed than most of the staid, polished females who typically sought entrance where he worked and lived—despite a cranky landlord.

Would *she* know just how he needed to be touched after a long, arduous day in the fields? Catching prey and earning his keep? Would *she* know which muscles needed attention? Where to stroke lightly, where to scratch with more pressure?

Would she serve his dinner in a timely fashion? And not make him wait—while she dithered about doing who knew what?

He stood and stretched, watching her unsteady approach as her slippered feet skated over the icy cobbles.

He'd never seen the newcomer before, but given the slush coating the road, the dark drizzle lining the outside of the windowpane and the very air beyond, she should have been "coated" herself. But nay, no cloak lined her shoulders. No bonnet her head.

No mittens her fingers, no scarf her neck.

What was this?

What manner of female would be traveling toward his begrudged lodgings in weather such as this without a shred shielding her against the fierce elements?

He gave a great yawn, his nose reaching toward the ceiling, his every limb and muscle lengthening with the move, as he circled and curled, settling back against the red velvet Mr. Chapman (his cranky landlord) had placed beneath the latest display—toppling one of the horse figurines that dared encroach on his slumber space.

"Barnabas! Have a care!" Chapman cranked from behind the counter. "Or I shall tan your furry hide."

Ho-hum.

"No-good rotten mouser, spending your days inside instead of at the warehouse or near the storeroom where you belong."

Humedy-hum-hum.

Tucking his tail beneath his chin, Barnabas slitted his eyes as a low rumble purred forth when the female skidded right into his front door, knocking it open and causing the noisome chime overhead to peal.

My, oh my. Eager, was she not—to feed and stroke his worthy self?

———◦⊂○⊃◦———

HEART POUNDING like a runaway team strapped to a rackety coach (which wasn't far from the truth), Lucinda Thomalin, sliding over the slick stones, barreled her freezing carcass toward the first—and only—shop still showing signs of habitation late this wretched eve. Pray God CHAPMAN & SONS promising HATS AND HOSIERY, GLOVES AND GOODS also provided safety to scared, single travelers.

The light whispering from the lanterns along the street feeble at best, motion in the large display window, visible even through the ice-crusted panes, nevertheless let her know help resided within—*if* she could get the door barred behind her swift enough. Keep out the terrors that had chased her thus far.

The cold, humid air suffocated like a grim haunting her lungs. Straining breaths panted from her as she raced, fast as she dared, over the dangerous cobbles intent on snagging a numb toe.

With every other establishment dark and locked tighter than a miser's trunk, the promised beacon of shelter on this bone-chilling, confidence-killing night drew her frozen self through the gloom. Slippers slithering over the dangerous surface, she slipped across the abandoned street with ungainly desperation as though she had wings on her back instead of the muck and mud from the last miserable hours.

Why, oh why, had she chosen to travel so close to Christmas, and in such questionable weather?

Your pockets are empty, lest you forget.

Aye, that.

And the agency she corresponded with claimed two others had already been told of the position—and were to interview Monday the 28th. With Christmas on Friday, that gave her scant time to win her prospective employer's attention beforehand.

Lucinda had wagered everything on the gamble that if she were the first candidate the elderly Lady Simmens interviewed, would she—Luce—not have a greater chance of being hired as companion?

Being a silent extension to another crotchety,

homebound lady will have you stark raving mad,
plucking your toenails off inside a sennight.

"If that—that creature doesn't do it first," she
muttered, barely resisting the urge to glance over
her shoulder to see if it chased her yet, shoving
aside the internal discourse in the wake of fear.
And relief.

Almost...there...

Feet whirrying over another slippy patch,
desperate arms outstretched, she grasped for the
door.

Smashed into and shoved it open, slid past
and splatted, facedown on the hard floor just
inside, the small rug no match for her iced
slippers.

———◆———

ONE MOMENT, Brier Chapman was kneeling
behind the long counter, elbows-deep inside the
delayed shipment of holiday decor; the next, the
thud-crash blasting through the door—along
with the chill—had him scrambling to his tired
feet.

Chaos erupted into his shop on the frozen
heels of the tart rubbing her bum—and showing
off an unseemly amount of "lower limb" (no man
worth his weight would ever so much as think *leg*
in the presence of a lady; even if he doubted this
one could claim such status).

"My gracious garters." Shaking what he could

see of her sodden, bare head as though stunned, she slowly placed her hands beneath her and pushed her torso upright. "That smarts."

"Here now." He rounded the corner of the long counter and rushed toward her, ready to rush her soggy, no doubt sordid, self straight back out the door and into the freezing night—despite the reluctance that weighed his shoulders at the thought. No one should be abandoned on such a dismal eve so close to Christmas. "I should have locked the door and pulled the curtains. We are no longer open. You must leave." *Now. Before my good sense goes the way of the sun and I let you stay the night.*

The last time sorrow for one in a similar plight on a stormy night gained the upper hand and overrode his common sense, he'd come downstairs the next morn to find the cot not mussed by slumber. And a significant amount of carriable inventory pilfered. Gone. Goods stolen into the night along with the skinning strummer.

It had taken weeks to regain equilibrium in the account books, far longer to recover his pride.

Damn doxies.

Ever since winter had set in, with its stout chill, bobtails had been banging their way inside many an afternoon, trying to get warm before—and during—the hours they plied their dubious trade. Three-penny uprights, with their hollow gazes and nose-wrinkling stench, invading the interior of the shop his family had minded for decades.

Why, just last week he'd had to chase away a "miss" *and* her prig who had attempted to make merry on the rug right in front of his latest display... The one he'd set up with painstaking care, despite the help from his laze-about "assistant", Barns.

And if it also made him lonely, seeing the two bodies intertwined in a shocking array of limbs (and yes, nearly bare legs), then what of it? At eight and thirty, Brier Chapman had known the love of a good woman for a wondrous but far too brief time, his dear Alice perishing along with their scrawny infant shortly after his birth. Though nine years had passed since Brier saw them both laid to rest and his heart had mended best it could, he couldn't stop his body from—on occasion—*yearning*.

But not for a tart, he reminded himself, gaining a better look at the offal the street had coughed up: long, straggly hair strewn over dirty shoulders of a dress that had seen better *years*— not just days; skirts splattered and ripped, one stocking drooped clear to her ankle, the limb above besmattered with filth. And was that blood?

He hardened his heart against the tempting array of sprawled limbs and ice-crusted dress. A streetwalker should know to attire herself better. He knelt, fingering the fine fabric, weighing its texture, assessing its weave and composition as only a buyer would, despite the sludge that spoiled it now. Nothing like what he'd seen on the others. Not the most expensive fabric, by any means, but certainly something a nightbird wouldn't bother with, not during winter. *Without a cloak.*

Doubts began creeping—

Nay. Thoughts of the last time he gave in to weakness and sheltered a stranger firmed his resolve—that and the chaffing he'd suffered from his brothers. He'd not be disadvantaged again. "You must go. Leave, madam."

Quickly, please. Before I inquire as to your disheveled state and lack of overclothing.

She ignored him. Scrambling even now, reaching toward the door with a flurry of panic out of proportion to the mild ire he'd exhibited.

"Quick, douse the lights!"

What? "Come now." He roughened his voice. "Be off with you."

She lunged for the doorknob, fought the latch that tended to stick in wet weather. "Bolt the doors! Rapidly now."

"Miss? You must be off."

"N-nay!" she panted. Fear or exhaustion? "Heed me, please. Keep it out!"

"It?" Curiosity slowed his haste to send her away. That and her proper speech. Not something he'd heard from the prior birds who'd pecked their way inside.

"The monster. The beast. He's been—"

"Stop that." Brier strode forth, beyond irritated with himself for not latching the doors sooner, locking *her* out. He'd only left the door unlocked because a good customer—a marquis' wife, in fact—had sent round a note, saying her spouse would be by to retrieve a recently arrived order after his other commitment this evening, if he could. Something must have delayed the Marquis, because Brier had seen neither hide nor hair of the reliable, if notorious, lord (whispers abounding about a house of delights Lord Blakely owned—but not something Brier had first-hand knowledge of, so 'twas easy to discount the rumors).

He reached her side, intent on shoving her outside—no room for weakness, he reminded himself, irritated all over again when he caught her scent: the soft, wholesome fragrance of rosewater she had no business wearing.

And he had no business noticing. Inhaling. *Sniffing*, even—by damn—trying to get impossibly closer even as he nudged her aside to wrench the door open against the blasting wind. "*Out*, I say."

"Have you not ears? There is danger afoot!"

BARNABAS EYED THE PAIR CURIOUSLY.

The wet woman he hoped would stay—at least long enough to fondle his furry self. The taller, broader man he'd lived with for years. The calm, sometimes cross, proprietor of this establishment—Barnabas's place of employment—the man who rarely smiled, yet never raised his voice.

But was certainly raising it now. "Be off with you, woman! This is no place to ply your wares, and your skinny arse is dripping everywhere!"

"Quick! Bolt the door." The female put her back to it and frantically scraped her feet for purchase, trying to shove it closed. "The key! Where is it?"

Barnabas watched with something akin to wonder as the two grappled over the door. Fighting each other every bit as much as the howling wind.

"Rrreow." *Close it, you loons. That blast of wind just gutted two candles.* Granted, they'd been almost burnt to puddles, given how late the hour, but still.

"Please leave, madam. *Out.*"

They jostled. Frozen rain and sleet pelted inside.

"There is something fiendish out there—and it is after me!"

"You are befuddled. Have you been tippling?"

"Merrow." *She's not befuddled. I see him.*

"You think a soaker would speak so clearly? Bolt the door, you bufflehead!"

"Not"—his man grunted—"until"—fought back the female dervish—"you're...beyond it!"

"Mew." *He's out there, I tell you.* "Merrow!"

The female whirled on Mr. Chapman, grabbed hold of his shirt between neck and shoulder and *shook*. "If you do not want my death on your conscience, quit being an idiot and help me."

With an aggrieved huff, his man finally stopped battling woman and door. "There is no one out there. Much less after you."

"Rrooeewwwl." *His eyes are glowing. Do you not see?*

"There is!" She released him and shouldered the door until it thumped shut. Wilted down in a *plop* of wet female and fabric, seating herself against it in a shivering huddle.

Mr. Chapman grunted at her. "Woman, I—"

"Yowl!" *Pay attention to me!*

The glowing eyes came closer through the night causing Barnabas's fur to stand on edge.

The cat, wearied of arguing humans disturbing his slumber, narrowed his gaze on the newest arrangement of goods: his man's most prized delivery for the holiday season.

Barnabas promptly batted first one and then a second piece straight to the floor.

The resulting raucous far more—and far more effective—than he'd expected.

"ME-OW!

2

CARRIAGE CACOPHONY

C-R-A-S-H!

The sounds of shattering pierced the air and blazed up Lucinda's spine.

She shrieked. The high-pitched yelp rang in her ears even as her body shuddered. Had the monster broken the window-panes? Come after her despite—

"Not the horses!" The man hovering over her shoved home the bolt—finally!—and lunged toward the bow window several feet from where she hunkered behind the stout door. "The carriage too? Barnabas, you bloody ingrate!"

"RRRreoowwww!" A spry brown-striped tabby with a fuzzy white belly launched itself off the man's back and into her lap.

"Barnabas! Damn back claws..." The grumbling continued a few feet away, but Luce ignored it. Too intent on the purring, warm bundle rubbing against her frozen hands. When had she lost her gloves?

Oh, somewhere between the two carriages smashing into each other; you and others flinging hither and yon; seeing the dead, broken bodies, the blaze of light; oh, and being chased within an inch of your life, mayhap?

Loud purrs rumbled forth, the comforting vibration better than a roaring fire would have sounded right that moment, helping her focus on something other than the terror that even now raced through her veins, made it difficult to inhale without gasping and grasping for air.

"Mew."

"Don't give me a dainty little *mew*," the man complained in a voice she could not but help respond to—no matter how inappropriate—the deeply husked tones warming her little corner, calming her storming heart as much as the friendly feline. "You rotten piece of good-for-nothing whiskers."

Purrrrrrrrrrrrrrrrr.

"Oh you are a sweetheart, are you not?"

She wasn't alone. She was safe—for the moment. And her benumbed fingers now had a purpose (other than fighting the man over the dratted door): she sank them into soft fur.

"My horses and carriage," he groaned, his voice quieter than it had been. "Why the horses, Barns? Why? After ignoring them since they pranced into the store, why now? And you, not bestirring yourself to catch a single rodent in ages. Should just stop feeding you. Boiled chicken...shredded turkey...sliced roast... Spoiling your sorry arse, I am. This is what befalls us both..."

Beyond the confines of the shop, the storm raged.

The cat bumped into her chin and Lucinda moved her fingers from stroking its sides to attack its fuzzy little head, around the ears, between them, and then beneath its jaw—which brought forth the loudest rumbles yet.

As the man busied himself maligning the cat and picking up large pieces and smaller shards, Luce glanced about the shop, the light meager but sufficient to reveal a striking number of goods, arranged invitingly. Closed, waist-high cabinets marched around the perimeter, with rows of shelving above that reached to the ceiling. Various-sized round tables dotted the floor throughout. Everything she beheld affirming exactly what had been promised from outside: an array of hats, gloves, stockings and such, bolts of fabric and a myriad other personals and household items that any other time she would enjoy perusing.

But the man's broad shoulders had snared her attention.

Now that he was no longer being an obstinate

knave, intent on thwarting her efforts, she could not help but admire his appeal.

His warmth, she still remembered as they battled side by side before he relented. But the dark-as-night disheveled hair, she just now noticed, thick and barely brushed with grey above his ears.

His task nearly done, the larger pieces all gathered, he sat back on his haunches and stared at the large empty spot on the display level with his head. Which appeared to be a good portion, centered in the wide window. His firm jaw, temptingly touched by evening bristle, angled in such a way that thoughts of exploring him made her quickly thawing fingers prick with more than the return of feeling.

Wind rattled a couple panes of the window, but the more she studied his large form...the more her heart and body distanced from the distresses of the last hours, the more an odd sort of contentment settled over her like a comforting blanket. "Horses, you said," Luce ventured, loath to bring his ire back to her, but curious nevertheless. "What did your cat break? Is there any chance of repair? For your display, if not for sale?"

"None whatsoever." All fight had gone out of him, it seemed. Serene acceptance coated his tone. He breathed deep, then pushed off the floor to head toward the back of the shop. Moments later, he returned with broom and dustpan. After a glance at her, a derisive chuckle and shake of his head when he noticed the cat now curled in her lap, he set to work sweeping the large chunks and finer pieces into the bin.

"You, no doubt, will think I respond all out of proportion as a matter of course." He sighed and she took feminine pleasure in watching the muscles of his shoulders stretch the fabric of his shirt—no jacket nor properly tied cravat hiding his neck this eve, she noted, which lent credence to his claim of the store being closed.

"These horses were a new design, arrived last month, with one broken during shipment, so that delayed things while I waited for the replacement. Four matched whites, you see, with such a sheen it could mirror your countenance; they even came with wreaths about their necks, dried greenery woven with ribbon and tiny gold baubles. On a lark, while waiting for the replacement one lonely night, I added a small wooden pole across the lead pair's chest, leather straps and traces from some scraps and connected the team to the sort of fabled carriage one would expect described in a fairy story..."

Did he realize he said *lonely*?

"More fool me, as that piece was irreplaceable —the carriage I scrounged from a trunk—something my grandmother had as a child, and thanks to my twaddy idea"—he gestured to the broken pieces he'd gathered—"since everything was strapped together, it's gone now too. Even jested with a couple customers earlier how Prinny himself would be jealous if he did but see it. Would want to commission something just as fantastical for his own use, certainly not above prancing through London himself.

"No help for it now." He stood, dusting his hands off against his trousers. Then he speared her with one pointed finger. "Stay put. Your slippers are no match for a sharp shard and the last thing I need is you bleeding on my floor."

Before she could take umbrage, he finished with, "Wait here until I can get things swept up and the floor wiped clear."

So he wasn't intent on casting her back outside? Into the raging rain?

The cat bumped her fingers again, making Luce realize she'd stopped petting, had thought he'd gone to sleep. Evidently not. She renewed the scratching beneath his chin and along his jaw; kitty renewed his loud purring.

Now that she was starting to thaw, silent and still for the first time in hours... Now that the terror of being attacked and mayhap eaten or killed was fading, aches and pains, bruises and scrapes started poking at her from everywhere: a pounding upon her forehead; a twinge in one ankle; a dull throbbing along her face; a dreadful *ack!* in her sit-upon, showing how very hard she'd landed earlier. Needles pricked her fingers and palms as they lost the rest of their frosty numbness.

Then the man was back, with a damp cloth, wiping the floor, gathering any smaller pieces his prior efforts had missed. "I regret your irreplaceable memory was destroyed," she told him. "You won't rout Barnabas over the mishap, will you?"

Should you not be more worried about yourself?

The man snorted. "That lazy ingrate? Who would I converse with if I tossed his useless arse out on the cobbles?"

The task finished, he walked past the counter, made a few noises in the nether regions of the shop disposing of the rubbish, she supposed. Then he returned—and surprised a silent squeak out of Lucinda when he extended his hand to her.

"Come now," he encouraged in that deep husk that warmed her every bit as much as the cat. "If I won't toss his pitiful carcass out, neither will I launch you back into the storm."

Not tonight, she sensed though it remained unsaid.

She hugged Barnabas to her middle and lifted her hand, swallowing down a moan when his warmly wrapped around it.

"Steady now?" He hauled her to her feet and didn't release her until she gave a nod. "Shall we get you dry and warm? Possibly something to eat?"

And *then* he would cast her out? His conscience assuaged?

No matter. She would take every second of

safety he might be willing to grant, and not worry about anything beyond until she had to.

"Please. I would be ever so grateful."

SHOULDN'T HAVE TOUCHED HER.

Brier fisted his hand at his side, and only just barely avoided wiping his palm across the thigh of his trousers in a hopeless effort to rid himself of the strange, lingering *sense* of her upon his skin. Instead, he confirmed the door was locked and bolted—at her begged behest—and at her urging also checked the one in the back. The plain door that led to the alley where he received deliveries.

Unwilling to open his upstairs lodgings to a stranger, no matter how alluring she smelled— he made a mental note to catalog her scent and share the constituents with his sister; Rose was forever playing with perfumes and scents, had quite the knack for it actually. His eyes glancing over to the selection of hand-painted attar bottles adorning one shelf, he led his visitor toward the storeroom in the back.

An eight-foot windowless square with naught but a long curtain bunched at one end of an elevated pole to shield it from sight when drawn, the room functioned as his catch-all, one wall populated with half-filled crates of merchandise, the opposite lined by a cot, currently piled with sundry items of his trade (things he had not the time nor inclination to find true homes for, or to return to the shelf or basket from whence they came). His desk resided in the middle, an oil lamp he'd lit earlier gave off sufficient light.

Once he had her seated at the desk he used for accounting and grabbing a quick bite during shop hours, he unwrapped the meal he'd brought down earlier, but hadn't stopped to eat, and laid it out before her: two thick slices of bread, three slimmer slices of roast and a chunk of cheese. "It's not fancy, but filling."

She started to reach for it, then stopped. "My hands." She flipped one over and then the other, studying the abrasions upon her palms. Fingered a broken nail. Then she lifted tired eyes to him. "I need to wash them first."

"Certainly. One moment." Feeling the burn of her gaze upon his back, he charged from the storeroom and up the narrow staircase, quickly retrieved a wash-basin, cloth, several towels for she was soaked clear through, and a clean chamber pot. (What good proprietor only had one?) At the last moment, he thought to add a tool to smooth her nails. Then he stomped down the steps back to her.

It wasn't eagerness that fired haste into his feet, not eagerness to see her, certainly. Nay, never that. 'Twas only the—slight—fear that she had already filled her pockets and escaped.

But nay, she slumped back in the chair, head resting upon the wall behind her, no bonnet, simply straggling hair, slowly drying around the edges, strewn down her shoulders and one arm, eyes closed, hand resting heavily upon a curled Barnabas who glared up at Brier as though to chide his master for how long he'd been gone.

As he came in, she blinked open weary eyes.

"I'll leave this here for you." He knelt and placed the chamber pot within sight but out of the way, near a corner. Rising, he placed the nail board, cloth and water upon the desk. The three towels he stacked beside, wishing one of his sisters had left clothing behind, or that he'd retained something of Alice's. "You'll no doubt want to"—did one say *strip* to a stranger?—"remove your sodden things and dry off. I'll retrieve a shirt—"

"No! Nay." Vigor returned to her tired gaze, nettlesome awaredom creeping in as well. "That is not necessary. The towels will do nicely and the food smells heavenly. Thank you."

So perhaps he would not forage his wardrobe upstairs for something she could wear. Not until he had time to discern her character.

But she smells divine.

As if that determined morals. Or mitigated potential thievery.

"Take whatever time you need. Call me when you're done and I'll see to your wounds." He nodded toward her bare hands.

"That has the ring of a man inconveniencing himself." A half-hearted smile tilted her lips.

"You no longer think me a bedlamite in need of immediate rousting?"

"That has yet to be decided. But I no longer think you a nightbird here to peck at my pockets and bring your unwashed wares where they were not invited."

No destitute mutton cat, this.

Nay, for now that he'd evaluated her, 'twas obvious whatever had made her flee, it had brought about true fear. Her manner, her elocution, it all bespoke refinement. Some sort of education.

Most of all, she wasn't leering at him through bleary, street-toughened eyes or granting him come-hither smiles through broken or blackened teeth, trying to work her wiles on his susceptible self. Although, even if she had been, at this point, after realizing whatever "monster" her imagination had figmented had scraped more than her palms raw, Brier suspected he'd grant asylum.

For how long, though?

That was the question.

3

A CHRISTMAS CONVENIENT?

———◦———

LUCINDA WATCHED her reluctant rescuer draw the curtain, giving her what privacy was to be had. Once she heard the solid thump of his footsteps retreat, the wary clench of every muscle released at once. Left her sagging into the chair, against the wall. Made it an effort to lift her head.

Food.

Though chilled from the outside in, the scent of bread and beef roused an appreciative rumble from her middle. "So unladylike," she chided.

Reaching over the kitty in her lap and skipping the cloth, she plunged her hands into the wash-pot to a loud sigh of relief. She'd worry about finding clean water to rinse the rest of the filth later, but for now, just being able to scrub beneath each of her jagged fingernails and gently wipe the dried dirt from the abrasions at the base of her palms helped sooth the ragged edges of her exhausted soul.

Little tags of skin pebbled beneath her fingertips. Made her stomach give a queasy lurch.

Had she fallen? Landed on her hands? She didn't recall.

Barnabas stood and stretched, his back arching, his tail flicking against her chin just before he hopped up to the desk. His gaze flickered, head turned toward the oil lamp—

"Oh no you don't, young man." Dodging the cloth and towels once more, she picked up the mischievous tabby, wet hands and all, and placed him on the floor. "Go along with you. No more knocking things off, not tonight."

He gave her a baleful glare and contorted, immediately set to licking every drop she had dared to transfer to his pristine person.

A short while later, after tending to the worst of her nails, making use of the chamber pot and tucking it out of sight, again washing her hands —this time thankful for the clean cloth—and using the topmost towel to blot her face, arms and neck dry, she applied herself to the meal. Plain but hearty fare that satisfied far more than the dainties her previous employer served in the guise of "elegance" that Lucinda always suspected were more to hide how extravagantly cheap the cantankerous, contradictory woman had been.

Startling how quickly both alertness to her

limbs and clarity to her mind returned midway through the repast. In between tearing off tiny bites for the feline who had reclaimed his perch upon the desk—on the opposite side of the lamp, she noted—Luce found herself sitting up straighter, the fatigue and fear receding as though to make room for worry to come marching in.

To distract herself more than anything, she swallowed and called out, "Mr.... Chapman? Or perhaps his son? You may return now."

The curtain slid open mere seconds later, alluding to his nearby presence. He nodded at the half-empty plate. "Good. Keep eating. I thought you might skip nourishment and fall upon the cot straightaway, spend the night in Nod. But you need to revigour and strengthen every bit as much as rest and slumber. When is the last time you ate?"

"This..." It hadn't been that morning. Her remaining funds being hoarded so she could pay for lodgings upon her arrival and refresh herself before her upcoming interview. "Nay, last..."

He took a seat on the cot, at ease—as though he were not counting the moments until he could be rid of her—his knees spread, hands clasped between them as he leaned forward. He frowned at her. "Do not tell me you have not eaten since yesterday."

She lifted one shoulder in a shrug. What else

could she say? The last two weeks, since her
employer's death, had been fraught.

"You aren't a tart." He said that as though it
had been in question. And 'twas the second refer-
ence he'd made toward such. Was it still in doubt?

"You sincerely think me a *convenient*?" A
gentleman's amorous plaything? She surged to
her feet. "I should say not!"

"Mrrrr-O-W!"

The man's strong face softened in a smile.
"Seems Barnabas agrees. Your name, then?"

"Miss Thomalin." She came round the desk,
to give him a polite curtsy—whether he deserved
one or not. "Luce—"

"Loose?" He chuckled, transforming his
features from angular to inviting. "Did we not
just agree—"

"Not a *wanton*, you stubborn man. *Lucinda*,"
she said with asperity, giving his shoulder a light
punch, then hissing when she realized how sore
the back of her hands. "Lucinda Most-Assuredly-
Not-a-Tart Thomalin. Originally from London.
Most recently employed in Brighton."

"Employed?"

"As a lady's companion, lest you let your tart-
filled mind go in other, more base directions."

"It hadn't. Not just then." The smile he gave
her was mischievous—and just a shade naughty.
What manner of shopkeeper had she barged
upon? "The question was pure curiosity, I assure

you. For I have not personally known an unmarried London female who was 'employed' in anything other than..."

"Bed sport?"

He gave a quick nod, his cheeks above the bristle turning ruddy.

"Then mayhap you have not known the *right* sort of women."

Embarrassment ceased as his features hardened once more. "Mayhap I have simply not known *enough* women."

How she wanted to inquire over that intriguing statement. "You speak with such candor," she told him, unsure whether she was trying to direct the conversation into more mundane areas or not. "'Tis quite invigorating, I confess."

"Doubtful." He pointed to the uneaten portion behind her. "If you're feeling invigorated, 'tis likely the beef."

She gave a snort of laughter, even as she shook her hand, her stinging fingers protesting.

He scooted to the far edge of the cot and gestured to the open area beside him. "Here. Sit next to me. Let me assess the damage."

"Damage?"

He pointed to her ungloved hand.

"Ah." She debated but a moment before launching forth a flirt of her own. "But sitting beside you, sir, would be ever so forward given how I have now introduced myself but you have yet to return the favor."

He acknowledged the rebuke with a slight smile. "You are correct. In one sense, I am neither the Mr. Chapman nor his sons you referred to, for that was my great-great-grandfather and offspring, until a decided change in fortunes, ah —*circumstances*," he seemed to correct. "Never you mind, for I am, for the most part, the current proprietor of our fair establishment." He stood, offered her a regal nod and then resumed his seat. "Brier Chapman, at your service.

"And to clarify something of import"—he gave the bottom of her skirt a light tug, encouraging her to join him—"that is Brier with an E-R at the end, not the commonplace A-R."

"Heavens. Neither of us should wish to be *common*, I am sure."

"'Twould be a dastardly grievance, I have no doubt. Now give me your hand."

Sitting next to him, even upon something as rudimentary as a cot was absurdly easy; placing her hand within his, allowing him to inspect her skin was most assuredly not.

"No doubt you think me owdacious and given over to histrionics." Babbles burst forth, as though her tongue was determined to distract the rest of her from how quickly his soft, exploring touch banished the sting from her skin, the lingering ache from her bruised posterior. "But I can assure you I am not. My mind is most sensible, as those who know me would attest. My manner somewhat somber—"

"That would be a shame," he murmured, turning her hand over to inspect the back, as she bit down on the hiss of pain when he ran one finger over a swollen knuckle with care.

"A shame? Why?"

"A miss such as yourself should not take pride in being somber."

"I should— *She* should not?"

"'Tis a crime. An unpardonable sin."

"Unpardonable? A *sin*? Surely you speak nonsense to distract me." With a steady tenderness she would not have expected from him the first few minutes of their brangling acquaintance, he placed her hand upon his thigh, just above the bend of his knee, and reached for her other.

Oh my, oh mercy. Breathing had never been of such import, nor focusing on thus as it became in the next few seconds, as she fought every urge within her to tighten and flex her fingers when the warmth of his body rose to infect hers.

Infect? You make him seem a virulent being full of vile intent.

Nay, not that. Never that. "Ah-*hem.*" Her breath caught in her lungs as she forgot to focus beyond where he surveyed the torn skin. "Mercy me."

"Aye?" He glanced at her from beneath dark brows, his shaded eyes alit, but not in the fearsome manner of the creature who had stalked her winded steps. Nay, Mr. Chapman's eyes were lit with something she couldn't quite discern.

Interest, you tart. You recognize it well enough. Now that he's not shoving you back out in the sleet and slurry, he's interested. You're just afraid of it.

Was she? Not ever having known the taste of a man's lips upon her own, nor that of his bare-fingered grasp upon hers...

See there, loose Lucinda?! Her inner voice practically cackled. *You went from interest to kissing!*

True. For despite the horrid afternoon and wickedly frightening night, all of a sudden savoring such illicit touches was *all* she wanted to think about.

"Surely, a sin," he confirmed as though there were never any doubt. "For someone as alluring and bloomy as yourself should never be considered somber."

Bloomy? She'd not thought of herself as attractive as spring flowers, as fresh and unspoiled as new growth in years. Perhaps a decade or more. To hear him spout such now? Did he play her false? Seek to woo some desperate non-tart into his bed with such drivel? Or did he, mayhap if miracles were shining down upon her, see past the tired, ennui-riddled companion to the sprightly woman within? The one who yearned daily to bloom in truth, right past the staid chignon weighing down her hopes and nape every bit as much as the drenched dress did her weary frame?

Too tired to attempt to decipher his intent tonight, she forced a wan smile, reluctantly slid her trembling fingers from his beguiling grasp where they wanted to linger, fisted them and crossed both arms in front of her chest. "And you accuse *me* of tippling? For shame, Mr. Chapman. For you, sir, most certainly must have imbibed sufficiently this eve to cast such clouds upon your clarity. Not if you think I would succumb to such sprouted drivel."

BRIER LET HER RETREAT. For now.

Didn't think it wise to mention the rousing bruise flaring upon her cheek and jaw. He hadn't noticed it earlier, when her face was flushed with exertion and fear, but now? The swelling was unmistakable. He was surprised she hadn't remarked upon the pain herself.

Also surprised she hadn't mentioned the pounder that had to be pressing upon her forehead, given the way she occasionally squinted.

Neither had he once witnessed her placing those sweetly trembling fingers upon her jaw or the side of her face—the ones that gave evidence his touch affected more than himself—nay, she had tucked her hands away and armored herself against any further inspections. As to the swelling upon her face, mayhap so much had happened this eve it had failed to knock upon her consciousness.

"I have some ointment upstairs." He pushed off the cot—with more reluctance than he would have expected a mere twenty minutes ago. "I'll retrieve—"

"You should not." She gathered her skirts close, tucked them beneath trim hips and gazed out toward the public shop area. "I should be off now. Surely, the threat since has left?" Her voice rose, denying what was meant to be a statement. "I must find a room. A—"

He knelt before her, rested his knees upon the hard floor and decided not to chide himself when his arms edged along the sides of her legs, his thumbs resting lightly near her waist—his longer fingers—drat their determined hides—settling, ever so carefully, mightily close to her hinderlands.

"Shush. You will not be leaving. Not tonight, possibly not tomorrow—not with the way the freezing rain continues to fall." If he were lucky, the cobbles would be iced to within an inch of their life, leaving the two of them cocooned within, without a single customer or reminder of the world outside to mar this unexpected interlude.

This close, the scent of her, deeper than the comforting, spicy fragrance he'd appreciated earlier, perhaps her own personal aroma, reached through his unsuspecting nostrils and gripped his innards hard. Made it a chore not to grip her plump posterior and haul her closer.

"But my interview." Fidgets overtook her calm demeanor, arms uncrossed, fingers began restlessly plucking at the fabric gathered in her lap. "I must go. Cannot remain here—"

He leaned back, giving her room to panic, his heart pounding harder than it had a right to. At the thought of her leaving? Or at her nearness?

A staggered gasp escaped her lips. She held up several inches of dirt-caked material between them. "Stars and sadness, my dress."

He watched, barely avoided cringing as she stuck one bare, raw-looking hand through a massive gash in the skirt, her face falling when it came right through. Wiggled torn fingers and then quickly pulled her hand back, wiping off the grime on a petticoat. Ripped, also. "Argh." Dismay sighed from her. "It's totally ruined."

And she was only now noticing?

"You see why I bid you to remain? At least until you have sufficient rest and time to gather your scattered wits." And scattered belongings? For she had arrived empty-handed. "Come, share the rest," he coaxed, unwilling to wait for her agreement before gaining answers, "and I will listen without censure." At least, he would attempt to. "To start, why in the world would you travel on such a miserable day? And alone? Are you to meet with family?"

4

CHRISTMASTIDE
CONFESSIONS

———◦◦———

"Family?" The strained laugh erupted before Lucinda could stop it. She slapped a hand over her mouth and winced at the soreness in her palm. Lowering the stinging appendage, she schooled her countenance into the calmest, most bland appearance she could manage. The one she had perfected whenever her prior employer would complain about her servants, her neighbors, her gout or her gadfly-infested chickens (the poultry Lucinda tended on a daily basis, not a gadfly in sight). "No, sir. I am not here to meet with family. Lest you think to chastise further, 'twas sunny and serene when I set off this morn for the coaching station, the dark clouds not visible till halfway here."

"Your coach did not pause when things became dangerous?"

Dangerous was the scarcely there brush of his fingers upon her lighted, dirty person. *Dangerous* was how her insides reacted to his proximity. "Had the other carriage not careened into us, I daresay we would have made it here, wet but all in one piece. As for myself, I could do naught but hold on and hope for the best—"

"Hold on?"

"I..." She grasped to hold on to her rapidly disintegrating composure—had a man not family ever remained so near? Ever? "I rode up top to save coinage," she confessed.

"On top?" He swore and jerked back as though the coachman's whip had cracked over his head. "It isn't safe! How—"

"You think I do not know that—*now*?"

One hand at his side now, the other resting two scant inches from her trembling thigh, a muscle in his cheek flexed as though he strove to remain—or at least appear—calm.

"But if you did not travel toward family, then why? Why burden yourself so close to Christmas?"

"Employment, you wretch." Utterly wretched of him to tempt her woebegone feminine yearnings, the ones she'd buried as deep down as a deceased cherished pet in the cold and lonely ground. "You think feasible opportunities for lodging and employment bang on the doors for people like myself? They do not. At least two others—that I know of—interview for the job I aspire toward on Monday. I thought if I could get here early, that I could break all boundaries and present myself on Sunday, in the middle of the day, not too early for a call but presumptuous nevertheless. I could endeavor to secure the position for myself, showing diligence and effort, despite the calendar."

"So close to Christmas?"

"Correct. Abysmal timing for anyone seeking employment, I know. The agency bid me wait until after the new year, but I could have none of that. My last position paid but a pittance, though secure lodgings were included, adequate food as well, so I shan't complain. But I must find something else and soon."

"I cannot fathom you having difficulty. Finding a position, that is. You speak well. Underneath the stench of travel, you—" He bit his tongue.

"You cannot tell a woman she reeks." But the chuckle she released said otherwise. He thought her malodorous? After what all she had endured today, that embarrassing nugget was the least of her worries. "I grant you, *I do smell all horse-piss; your nose should be in great indignation.*"

He stared at her a moment, as though one of those (nonexistent) gadflies had landed upon *his* nose, then he threw back his head and laughed. Uproariously, to the point that she found herself smiling along and even lightly tapping one soggy slipper. "Well done, madam. Though you misquoteth the great Bard himself, you delight me. And I wasn't, *wasn't* calling you aromatically fetid, I swear. The opposite, in truth."

"Oh?" Dare she believe him? "'Underneath that stench, I...'" she prompted.

"You smell... I should not say more." In a fluid move she could only gape at, he was on his feet, standing farther from her than she might wish. He clasped his hands together in front of his chest and angled them downward. "Forgive me. I'm being totally improper. And toward a miss I only just met. Informally, at that."

"Hang formality," she braved. "I want to hear. Dear sir, just how do you perceive my travel-weary redolence?"

"Mer? Mer*ow*?" Seemed as though she wasn't the only one curious. A quick glance over his shoulder showing the satisfied—if impertinent—feline had re-situated himself directly before the plate of remaining victuals.

"Barnabas, hush," Mr. Chapman said without turning his head, an abashed grin her reward. "Forgive me if I say anything out of hand, Miss Thomalin. One can only converse with felines with so much wit and tact. I fear mine may have gone begging over the last months.

"You smell absolutely delightful," he astonished her by saying next. "Rose-water. A hint of vanilla. And something else, something soothing yet somehow spicy. I don't think I have ever scented anything so fine."

. . .

AND BRIER WOULD KNOW.

He'd sniffed a number of confections in his day. He thought of the throwaways, the slim glass scent bottles on display out front. The ones fine ladies purchased for their reticules or to try a new fragrance.

Mayhap he could give her—

He mentally shook himself. Nay. For that way lay too much danger. Far too much appeal.

"Where did you come from?" he asked, to shift things far away from toilet water and temptation. "Who are your people?" Perhaps he could discharge his duty by seeing her returned home? Or to her destination, if closer.

You really want her gone—still?

He should.

"Brighton. We left shortly after lunch, and were met with one delay after another, thanks to first a broken wheel and ultimately the weather. And then—then upon reaching London." That stark gaze rose to his once again, any mirth brought about from their exchange over scents and Shakespeare long dissolved. She bit her lips as though to stop either her words or their trembling, but the rest rushed out like a waterfall. "We were supposed to arrive just before dark. I was to get a room, ahead of my interview. Only the flash, the crash, the utter and complete destruction. Our coach, destroyed. The carriage that slammed into it—the people, the injured... The dead. The beast! Chasing"—her lips trembled yet again —"chasing after me. So I ran, ran like I haven't in years. Cannot believe I didn't fall or twist an ankle. Fall victim to the beast."

Like a child in the throes of a night terror, her entire body quaked. Perhaps if he listened—and she expunged the memories, they would lose their hold? He resumed his seat next to her, wishing, and not for the first time this eve, that he had a more comfortable settee or chaise in here, rather than the concave cot that was never meant for extended sitting. "Tell me, if you would, of this beast you fled."

When she hesitated, he placed one arm hungrily over her shoulders, damning the flare of heat that brimmed along his side. No time for that, now.

Not when his woman needed comforting.

So now she is yours?

As she silently snuggled into his side, he bit back twin groans. One of ill-timed desire; the other toward the nagging voice that made him face the unfathomable feelings of want and, aye, *possession*, gripping him the last few moments.

———— ❦ ————

She seems safe enough for the night.

What? Where had that come from?

Barnabas looked to and fro, narrowed his

feline gaze on his landlord and their visitor. Neither was talking, not with words, anyway.

Only with touches, with pets. Mr. Chapman brushed his fingers along her shoulder over and over, occasionally straining the tips up toward her neck and over her head.

Barnabas could nearly feel the touch himself. His fur rippled all along his spine. How he wished—

Believe I shall be off. I shall chase—er, check on, ha ha—her again soon.

Whose words were those?

Curiosity prompting his silent steps, Barnabas jumped down from the remnants of well-devoured roast (thanks to his sharp claws and equally sharp canines) and padded back into the shop. His hind legs easily propelled him onto his bow window napping nest, made appreciably bigger now that the niffling horses and such had been dispatched.

He stared out into the black night, his keen gaze seeing beyond the freezing mist. "Rrrrr-owww!"

In the act of leaving, the stranger with the glowing eyes turned back and faced Barnabas. *You hear me, do you not?*

"Meow!"

Fascinating, I had not known of this ability.

"Rreeow! Merrep?! Mew?"

Oh, what happened to her? The carriage emergence, you see. When they cracked together, she flew skyward, her face seeking a monstrous tree overhead. I managed to snare her mid-air, just as her head collided with the branch. Slumbered her, it did. Had no inkling she would wake so soon and hasten off.

"Rrrppow? Mwwrr?"

How did we know to be there? I still don't fully understand it myself, how my mustached companion knew to be on guard watching those four-cross-roads when the accident happened.

"Mrrow."

You agree with me, then? Madful notion, is it not? I blustered about it beforehand, thought it more of a lark than a true concern—and I was supposed to be doing my wife, Francy, a favor.

His visitor exhaled a resigned sigh.

Barnabas could sense, if not outright hear, that too. Magical monkeys and dancing mice (*before* he bit off their heads, that was) what astonishing delights had he discovered, thanks to this stranger?

Out of respect for Adam—he of the hideous mustache—we waited. I confess, I am anticipating the explanation of how he turned prophet overnight and knew that the evening hours of December 23, 1812 would prove disastrous for some—and if the Lord sees fit to bless the innocent—beneficial for others.

"Mrow. Rrrrrrrrrrr."

I am thankful she made it safely here as well. Watch over her, will you?

"Merr?"

Aye, you, little one. See that no ill becomes her, can you do that? I have much work to see to before the sun rises. But I shall return again, when I can, to ensure she has met no harm.

Once the fearsome stranger's back faced Barnabas... Once the booted feet pounded away into the night... Once nothing but silence met his ears over the slick of sleet and drips...the cat yawned and stretched, his front legs reaching far, individual claws extended, piercing the red fabric as his hind end and tail rose toward the ceiling.

"Hmmmmm-mmmm," the yawn exhaled pleasurably and he retracted his claws, gave his shoulders one more flick and stretch and curled into a tight ball.

———————◦———————

"I..."

Against his side, the bedraggled, bemusing female hesitated. Afraid he'd ridicule again?

"Go on now," Brier encouraged. "'Tis not my place to deride." Not now that she'd roused protective instincts every bit as much as a curious fascination to know everything about her. "I would hear your tale."

"After the accident..."

"Accident involving exactly what? Who and how many?" If she was exaggerating over a broken tongue or strap, then he would know not to put great store in everything she claimed.

"Our crowded stagecoach. Another coach and a fine carriage."

He winced. A number of innocents involved, then. "Go on."

"Aft-after the dead were separated, the injured being tended, I sought shelter beneath a tree. It had grown colder, was still raining."

"Injured. Did no one offer to see to your hands?" She looked down as though still surprised to find their scraped appearance.

Then she found his gaze again. Her pale eyes were luminous, but blue or green or in between, he knew not, needing more light to discern their color.

After licking her lips once, she said, "Not trifles. I talk of *injurious* injuries, sir. The sort that one may not recover from."

"Ah." Hard not to cringe in the face of that. "All right. What came after the calamitous event?" What started her feet upon their flurry?

"There was talk of securing another stage but not until morning. Several others—a man, woman and baby, and another couple with two children—walked off, seeking shelter someone said. I waited—huddled, more like—feeling useless. The men who separated the broken coaches had already barked at me to stay out of their way..."

Her voice grew inertious and he cupped her shoulder and gave a nod of encouragement, pleased when she continued. "I thought to accompany the families. At the time, that made more sense than standing there growing more drenched and dreary every second. I started in the direction they'd gone. Only they must have lived close by for despite my haste, I did not see them through the murk. But by now, someone else followed me.

"At first, I thought it was perhaps one of the rescuers, come to offer escort, but nay. No one called out for me to wait, yet I sensed someone shadowing my footsteps with ill intent. I looked over my shoulder, saw nothing, but walked faster. The next time I glanced behind me, a dark shape with glowing, enflamed eyes—like the evil one—hounded my footsteps." She spoke faster, agitation growing as she abandoned his embrace and rose to pace the small room. "No one was about. The streets deserted. Shops closed tight. But still, he—it—came after me, so I ran. Faster and faster—and faster again when he roared—"

"Roared? For the first time, I struggle to believe you."

"*Roared*, I say!" And he was glad to see her stomp her foot and hold her ground, despite the fatigue lining her features. "Regardless of the raging storm, I raced through the gloom like a desperate, only stopping once I saw your lights. Movement beyond your window—"

Her breathing had become a series of labored, fast pants, panic edging into her tone and gaze, so he sought to distract. "What of your valise? Your trunks?"

"I have only two bags—or, had. Both...lost... In the brabble of everyone attending the injured and themselves."

"What of the rest? Is that to be sent along?" After she secured employment, perhaps?

"The rest? There is no *rest*. No other..."

Which meant, astonishingly, no *others*, either. What was someone like her doing out alone this close to the holiday? All afrazzle? And still too damn tempting...

"No... More." Her empty, swollen fingers flexed.

"Nothing?"

Her eyes seemed to glaze over, no longer seeing him. "Gone. Every single thing... Gone."

'Twas the first time, despite her ragged condition and the wild tale she'd spun, he'd seen her eyes glisten.

Tears.

Understandable, heart-wrenching tears that shredded his resolve to remain unaffected. Uninvolved. "Clothing, I can help you replace." He gestured beyond into the shop, toward the wall of fabrics, the shelves of ladies' things just waiting for her perusal. She could choose what she needed tomorrow. Assuming she could sew, he could see her attired in a trice and at no cost to her. Otherwise, a dressmaker would be the first order of business.

What happened to not involving yourself?

The very concept of sending her back out to survive on her own was like glass piercing his chest. "What else is missing?"

What else could he help her replace?

Before seeing her to her destination, correct?

Brier growled inside. *Stubble it*, he told that annoying voice.

"Nothing vital to anyone else, or even myself, I suppose. Stockings..." A great sigh heaved from her chest. "My other dress. The better one I was to wear to my interview." She looked down at her feet and he could feel the stark tremble that bled through her limbs. "These were my only good slippers. My last employer didn't go out much, saw not the need for me to 'spend frivolously' upon walking boots."

Brier grunted. To his experienced eye, her only "good" slippers were now good for nothing more than the rubbish pile.

"My mother's Bible..." She was still counting off what was gone. "Father's cherished snuff tin... Grandmother's handkerchief." She gave a loud sob. "I swear I could still smell her when I lifted it t-to my nose. So what else is missing? Just my remaining memories...a min-miniature of my sister... 'Tis all I have left of her. Went missing shortly after she turned fifteen."

And I thought I was alone?

"I shall see you safe. Find you something fresh to wear. Bring another bowl, with warmer water this time. After a quick wash, a decent night's slumber, things will look brighter in the morn. I vow."

Just how do you propose to keep that promise?

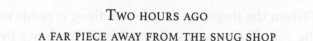

TWO HOURS AGO
A FAR PIECE AWAY FROM THE SNUG SHOP

"SHE'S GONE," the being who (formerly) referred to himself as The Beast gritted out in dismay. "The quiet one beneath the tree."

His companion dashed the persistent rain from his forehead, both their protective hats long since lost tonight. "Likely left with the others."

If wishes could only make it so. "No. She remained after they departed."

His companion and friend straightened, propped his hands on his waist and surveyed the surrounding destruction they sought to recure. "Then she lived nearby," Adam concluded in a tone no doubt meant to be convincing. "No need to be anxious over her whereabouts. We have more than enough to deal with right here."

"Nay again. The others hailed from the north, claimed it only a short distance to their destination. *She* did not accompany them today." The beastly one (for old habits were oft difficult to break) inhaled, nostrils flaring. "Seawater. I smelled it on her cloak, a hint upon her hair.

Unlike the others, she was on the stage from Brighton."

"Well, shit."

He inclined his head. "As you say. One of us needs to—"

"I know, I know." Rubbing a finger over a bushy, rain-slicked mustache, Adam huffed. "Given the lingering drizzle and time, it needs to be you, E. Can you still smell her? Track her by scent? Make sure she's all right? Doesn't succumb..." The heinous acts they were all too aware of the last few months didn't need to be named.

A second, intent inhale proved the truth of Adam's supposition. "Aye. I shall see to her."

Already, his powerful thighs shook with the need to chase after her, to ensure her safety, not have the death of one more innocent weighing upon his soul.

"Then go," his friend said. "We'll handle things here until your return."

A brief nod and he was off, storming through the dark, sodden night, surprised by how good it felt to escape the carnage behind, if only for a short while.

Felt good until he caught up with her only to discover a crew of rufflers and rogues had her in their sights as well.

As his friend would say, *shit*.

They'd reached the edges of the inner city, dark and dank in both fact and feel, not far from the river; not far from decent destinations. But now? Tonight? Evil would overtake her before she had a chance to flee beyond the threats. He paused, assessing, vexed that she was still racing ahead, but knowing he could overtake her—once this new danger was nullified.

There were seven, mayhap eight of them, cackling and arguing in the alley, deciding who would have her first.

Bile rose in his throat.

He could take two or three of them, likely four, on his own, but beyond that was risky. Especially if he didn't want to become a beast in truth and leave carnage in *his* wake tonight. Draw unwanted attention.

So he did the only thing he thought might work—allowed the creature within to surge forth, but not completely. Stopped just out of sight of the gang, opened his mouth and lungs and roared as if his life depended upon it.

Because he knew with certainty that hers did.

5

A COMPANION'S CONUNDRUM

———◆———

Barnabas was in heaven.

After his landlord saw the delightful—if dirty —female settled in the windowless room used for storage and such, Barnabas saw her coverings tucked in tight, felt the gleeful attention from dutifully petting fingers that paid the most exquisite attention to the top of his head, behind his ears and yes—oh merciful mounds of mice!— his chin!

Once she'd tended him to his enchanted, chin-thrumming satisfaction, he marched up the noisy planks and jumped up beside his man, who sat upon the edge of the soft rectangle with a besotted smile curving lips that were often far too straight.

Barnabas head-bumped against his shoulder.

"Rrreeeoww." *Don't let her leave.*

"How can we let her leave tomorrow, Barns? Risk never seeing her again?" Mr. Chapman removed his shoes and stood to unfasten his leg coverings before dropping down to sitting again. "If she interviews to be some old woman's companion..."

"Merrr." He bumped harder. *You need a companion.*

"Mayhap... I should try again? Hire her as assistant." The last one had been a nincompoop with numbers, causing his man all sorts of grief after each closing. "Not give her a chance to leave?"

"Mew." *Aye, we need to keep her.*

"But it isn't done." The leg coverings were tossed in a corner; after three days' wearing, Barnabas knew they would remain there until his landlord ran upon his last pair and would hire out the washings. If humans could only use their tongues! How much more efficient. "A female shopkeep? In the city? Am I really considering such a thing?"

"Pffft." *Retain her anyway. I need someone who gives good chinnies.* Barnabas flopped to his back, wiggling against the coverings alongside Mr. Chapman.

"We'd scandalize the whole street. The town. All of England, perhaps."

"Rrowl." *You're still not petting me! And I'm giving you belly opportunity and everything.*

"Or would we, perhaps, bring in more custom

than ever? It isn't unheard of, not in the country, I know. Mayhap town ladies might be drawn to the idea, men simply curious to see a working female in trade, one not a relative..."

Barnabas rolled over to his feet and placed his two front paws on the soft upper skin of his landlord's leg.

"But nay, then all would think she was a tart in truth, living here with me."

Barnabas stretched his paws, extended claws. And *pierced*.

"Aaaahhh! You ingrate!" With gentle care, his human pried the sharp talons from his weak skin and *ker-plopped* Barnabas on the floor. "I'm starting to think you, my friend, are totally useless as a mouser. Damn, Barns. That hurt."

"Mew." *Make it right.*

"Don't *mew* me, you ungrateful wretch." His man slid under the covers, pulled them up to his waist and sighed. Barnabas considered jumping up. But was peeved. With a flick of his tail, he turned toward the stairs. His landlord's words paused his paws though. "Mayhap... Mayhap I should consider courting the lass? It's preposterous. Outrageous. To consider such a thing after only mere hours' acquaintance? But if ever someone needed Christmas cheer, it is she. And mayhap so do I. Is that not why I spend my holidays here, avoiding family myself? Not wanting to burden them with my un-cheery mien?"

Mr. Chapman thumped and bumped beneath

the layers, as though unable to find a comfortable spot to curl up in. Barnabas turned about and rose up, lifting his front paws til he could peer over the edge. His man stared up at the ceiling. "Not to mention how I miss cuddling with someone who doesn't claw my thigh and avoids earning their keep." Was that another hit at his hunting skills? "I wonder if Miss Lucinda Thomalin has any talent with numbers or catching mice..."

Definitely a hit, then.

"Rowlll." *I shall show you my skills. With a herd of varmints beneath those covers if you don't mind your manners.*

His man gave a quiet chuckle, rolled over to his side and pointed to Barnabas. "If I keep her, you may just be out of a job."

Keep her? "Rreow? Merrowl!" *Is that not what I have been saying all night?*

———◦◦◦———

EARLY THE FOLLOWING MORNING, Brier tiptoed down the stairs, careful to stay to the right edge, not wanting the creaking boards to wake her—if she remained, that was. Not sure if he expected to find her eyeing him warily in the light of day or if he would be feeling the fool in five more treads, upon learning she'd snuffled goods and stolen off into the night.

He nearly tripped over the dead mouse at the

bottom of the stairwell. Smiled grimly to himself and whispered, "Not quite so useless, after all, are you, Barns?"

He hadn't seen hide nor fur of the thigh-piercing reprobate all morning. Unusual, for a feline that usually demanded his fill of both attention and victuals before deigning to leave the upstairs bedchamber.

At the storeroom curtain, Brier paused. Took an extra-deep breath to fortify the odd unease the silence beyond brought and slid the curtain aside.

The sight that greeted him proved neither so simple as an awake but wary female nor so disheartening as a missing one gone off into the night with all she could carry. For instead, Miss Lucinda Thomalin slumbered deeply, wrapped tight within the coverings he'd provided. Barnabas curled upon her chest and beneath her chin of all things, the cat's eyes narrowed at him as though saying, "Do not dare make a sound and wake my mistress."

Well now.

Well now, seemed his sometimes surly grudger of a cat had found someone worth snuggling.

The large bruise he'd noticed last night had riled full force on the side of her face and jaw. The sight of it lent further strength to her Banbury tale. For even had a crazed woman ripped her dress, rolled in the mud and demanded entrance for "safety" but really simple shelter and a full belly, he doubted one such as she would find a way to pound her own face into purpling.

On silent feet he approached the cot, bent and brushed his fingers along Barnabas's back and then stroked her hair away from her face. The feline gave a light *ptff*; the female barely sighed in her heavy sleep.

He straightened and watched them for several long seconds even though the presence of the dead mouse nagging for removal pecked at his heels every bit as much as his shop—and potential customers—prodded for opening.

No time to remain and ponder. No time to pause and enjoy. Not when dead rodents and retail beckoned.

Brier backed out, slid the curtain shut with quiet care, his heart humming a more contented tune than he could remember it playing in years.

———◦◦———

"Crush me, I cannot seek employment like this." Lucinda stared at her reflection in the afternoon light coming in from above the display, more than a little dismayed at the extent of the prior night's terrors upon her countenance. She flung herself from the bow window—after a single chuck beneath Barnabas's chin and whirled over to the counter where Mr. Chapman had spread open his account journal.

As he'd foretold last eve, the icy downpour had continued, keeping all but the most hardy and determined shoppers at home.

Small touches throughout the store hinted at the holiday and couldn't help but lift one's spirits, whether they be storm-dampened (his customers') or downtrodden (hers). Yet beyond the shop—the public area visible from the street windows—any reminders of the season were absent. His stockroom—and, she could not help but wonder, his lodging upstairs?—barren of holiday hints.

Visitors today had numbered in the single digits, and the loud bell over the door, as well as efforts to shake drizzle from umbrellas gave her time to escape, unnoticed, into the back if needed, on the few occasions she had approached and offered assistance. She didn't like feeling so beholden to him, promising to work for her keep, to pay him, reimburse him for everything. *I can cook, not fancy, mind, but basics,* she'd assured. *Clean your lodgings, the shop—*

Nay, he'd rejoined. *You will do no such thing. You will rest and recover and we will go on from there.*

Comforted at having a safe place to gather herself from the fright, unwilling to sacrifice her current safety out of foolish pride or spite, she remained, and ultimately spent most of the day staying out of his way while scrubbing at her dress, mending what she could and trying not to bemoan the lack of everything else. He'd given her one of his nightshirts to sleep in (horridly scandalous but so very welcome, nevertheless).

Not until he'd locked the door to the street and doused all but the front lamp he studied by had she felt free enough to venture forth and inspect the wares brimming in CHAPMAN & SONS.

Finding the hand mirror and thinking to gaze upon her features by the waning light outside had proved more a curse than a blessing. "I look no better than a bruiser."

He glanced up at her approach and gave her a thoughtful gaze. One she felt upon her person even more than the swelling weighing her face. "Perhaps not a bruiser," he said evenly, "point in fact."

She put the hand mirror down with a snap, gestured to the horrendous-looking cheek. "Then what would you call it?"

"'Bruisers' usually win. They are tops at fighting. While you—"

"Appear as though I lost."

His face scrunched in sympathy. "Heartily."

"Well, looking like a veritable brabbler, then"—a fighter—"I cannot go marching forth, interviewing for a position that requires gentility." Or could she?

"Mmm." He cocked his head and kept studying her face.

It took great effort not to look away, to look down, to lick her lips which tingled peculiarly beneath his regard. Took effort not to pinch color in her cheeks—to combat that of the bruising along her jaw and beyond. "Pray, what does that mean? *Mmmmm?*"

"That having lived with first my sisters and then my late wife, I am astute enough to know I should not tender an opinion on such a...potentially charged statement."

What? That she looked too brutish to follow through on her entire reason for coming to London? "Come now," she challenged. "Cowardice is not something I would attribute to you during our short acquaintance. Tender away..."

"Then, my dear Luce." Her name heaved from him as though an aggrieved sigh. "You cannot march forth. Not, I fear, as you appear this moment. On that, I must wholeheartedly agree."

"Agree? Wholeheartedly. Nay. You cannot." The wretch. Even now his somber tone, paired with the twinkle in his eyes, made her struggle against a chuckle. Because, of course, complete agreement by a man with a female was so very rare.

"Aye." He gave a determined nod. "I must. Fully and without reservation."

"Agree? It isn't done. I am certain of it."

"What? Concurrence?"

"Yes. It is quite horrid of you."

"I'm a brute."

"Of the most rotten sort."

"Should I... Disagree with you, then? Would that make everything aright?"

"Assuredly, you should. With verve and passion." *You brothel bait! How dare you banter blithely about—and with a man you just met?*

Surprisingly easily.

"Why, Miss Thomalin-alin-alin." Luce watched, wholly entertained, as he affected a shaky, high-pitch reminiscent of an aged woman —if she tippled and toppled and sounded the loon. He tottered back and forth behind the counter. "Do come in, dearie, for I have need of a bruising sort of companion. One who can shame rainbows in the sky with her very countenance, thanks to the field of flowers ripe upon her cheek.

"Greens and yellows and purples, oh my. I will not be able to take you anywhere!" His prancing footsteps paused and he brought one dainty hand up to his jaw, as though flourishing a handkerchief. Keeping the elderly voice and manner, he widened his eyes. Cocked his head. "Although... If one such as you were to be in my employ, could you not, mayhap fight off footpads and highwaymen? Why, alas! I could dither hither and yon to my aged heart's content and you, my dear—*you*, of the giant bruised jaw and puny-muscled arms—would you not be able to protect my virtue? I am in alt! In alt, I say. Why, I will hire you upon the nonce!"

By now, she was grinning and giggling so

much her sides hurt, cheeks pained from smiling —not to mention the stretched swelling. "Upon the n-nonce?" Chuckling so hard, she could barely speak, she asked, "What matter of nonsense do you spew?"

"I have no idea other than when you challenged me to respond with verve and passion..." Back to his normal, husky timbre, his response quickly banished the laughter lurking close to the surface. "I wanted nothing more than to bend you back over my arm and claim your lips with more passion than I have felt in the last decade. And would that not make me the most veritable of scoundrels?"

He slapped both palms upon the counter, his shoulders and head rising to their full and impressive height. "How could I even contemplate such? To take advantage of one dependent upon me, one within my care? *I* should be the one banished into the stormy wilds beyond the safety of the shop. Tomorrow is Christmas Day; I expect no one to trouble us. So you will have another quiet day to recover. I bid you good night."

With a gentle touch of his knuckles to the discolored bruise under discussion, he gave an abrupt nod and spun away, the sound of his feet pounding up the stairs two at a time no match for the pounding of her heart.

As his gentle touch spread from her cheek and jaw across her face and down to her toes...

As the laughter and the frivolous exchange left her breathless...

As she wished with everything in her that he had obeyed his first inclination and kissed her —passionately.

She might have missed out on the unexpected lifting of her heart and spirits, of the giddy, humor-induced tears that even now she wiped from beneath her eyes. Might have missed out on knowing the full extent of his unexpected mirth and flair for the farcical.

Might have missed out on how so very, very easy it was to converse with him, despite their short acquaintance.

But she would not have missed out on his kiss. Not for any of that.

Knowing that she had, uncertain whether the moment would present itself again, left a strange and gaping hollow in her chest.

6

A KISSING QUANDARY

———◦———

UNABLE TO SLEEP, unwilling to face his guest after their near-but-not-quite physical encounter, despite the hollow in his gut that reminded him he'd skipped dinner, Brier waited until hearing the clock chime eleven before he roused his sorry self from the disarrayed bedding and pulled his shoes back on—never having undressed in the first place, just flopping backward on the bed, forearm thrown over his eyes and a grimace adorning his lips the last hours...

As he revisited those precious moments with not-loose Lucinda, of the piercing blue eyes he'd catalogued the first time she'd ventured forth today—their brilliant, country-sky hue as firmly entrenched upon his senses as her scent. As her vibrant spirit.

In truth, he couldn't help but wish she were. Loose, that was. "And damn me for the thought."

Not since his dear Alice had he exchanged witticisms so freely with any female not a relation. Not once, in the last nine-plus years (or realistically, *eight* years, given that first year of deep, deep mourning, the days—and nights—of grief so acute he wondered at times if he would ever bluster his way through) had he longed to lock his lips against another's.

But now?

The minutes that had crept by since his escape—and that's what it was, he, a grown man, *fleeing* from desire. The interminable minutes that had both passed by in a flash yet yawned with excruciating slowness as he relived every nuance since the bedraggled package had first burst through his door and through his customary self-possession.

"Shredded that, she has."

"Mer?"

"*Mer*, indeed." He tugged the comfortable heft of Barnabas against his chest and fell back onto the mattress, mitigating his wince when eight or more sharp claws pierced his shirt as the cat made bread, scones and any other baked good he could think of out of his chest. Purrs roaring and rumbling through the night, the sweet sound all that comforted Brier on this dark eve.

His own conscience wouldn't let him sleep.

Regret? That he hadn't taken that longed-for kiss?

Relief? That he had fled before embarrassing them both?

"Either way"—he breathed out through the tiny, repetitive pin-pricks decorating his skin—"think I might be doomed. Doomed to lament, doomed to desire. What does it matter anymore?"

For tomorrow would dawn sure as certain, and once the swelling went down, Lucinda would be gone.

"Meow!" The claw-kneading stopped. The cat took two steps forward and swiped at his nose.

Left a streak of pain and one of blood—he noticed when he dabbed the back of his hand against it. "Damn it, Barns. I don't need to deal with your sulks on top of my own."

He rolled the cat off and bounded to his feet. "*I did not then entreat to have her stay; It was your pleasure, and your own remorse;*

"*I was too young that time to value her...*"

Shakespeare's words rolled through him, prompting the thought, *I am* not *too young to value her.*

So shall you entreat her to stay?

FOR ABOUT THE FORTY-SEVENTH TIME, Lucinda rolled over in the inward-dipping cot. Last night, she'd been too exhausted to notice much beyond the man, the cat—and the safety. Tonight?

Tonight, her entire body was a maelstrom of discontent. She'd woken this morning with her face aching abominably. Fingertip exploration had presented the swelling—and the touch had roused tenderness. But it wasn't until viewing herself in the hand mirror that the full truth of her injuries "hit" home.

If only she could remember better those dark moments after the crash. But nay, anytime she pressed her mind for memories, the dull ache lining her forehead riled into a seething beast itself.

Restless more for the absence of the kiss his last words had taunted her with than anything else, her lips tingling and stomach fluttering over the lack, she flopped onto her back and stared sightlessly at the ceiling. With the curtain pulled, and night decidedly descended, not a shred of light illuminated her surroundings.

When she'd listlessly returned to the storeroom after his precipitous exit, she'd found all manner of ribbons and a few surprising sprigs of greenery, along with a note:

Make these useful, if you're of a mind. Bring some holiday cheer to the back rooms. Be vocal if there exists anything else in the shop you could use.
~B

What a thoughtful, thoughtful man. He must have relocated the items and note onto the desk whilst she'd been exploring his shop. Rather than do as invited, after that blood-thrumming exchange of theirs that ended so abruptly, she'd fingered a spool of ribbon and let a lifetime of regrets, of missed opportunities flow out of her mind via the silent leak of tears down her cheeks until deciding enough was enough.

So, after consuming the food he'd brought down earlier, wandering around the empty shop, hoping he'd return—to no avail—she'd set herself the task of healing sleep.

"Unsuccessful task," she muttered through clenched teeth.

The soft tread of near-silent footsteps met her ears and relaxed her jaw. She eagerly held her breath for more. Was he approaching her? Finally! Would he push aside the curtain and finish what he'd so carelessly tossed temptingly forth?

A kiss...

It would be her first. The first that would matter, of a certainty.

The inept fumbling of another twelve-year-old, when she was still a girl not yet budding into womanhood did not count.

But nay, her heart crashed down when the footsteps never neared, going the opposite direction, in fact. And moments later? When the back door opened, albeit on quiet hinges, and she heard him talking in a low voice with—

Luce tore from the bed and tugged the curtain aside a few inches to make room for her hungry ear...

Heard him talking with a *female*.

In the middle of the night? When all was quiet beyond the shop. Silent beyond the two murmuring voices.

The elegant tones of the feminine one making Luce's stomach clench. Did Mr. Chapman yet woo another?

And what of it? Do you think a flirt or two means he is wooing you?

Well, no. Not entirely. No matter that one might hope—

Are you not to interview in two scant days and take yourself off? The life of a woman dependent upon the largesse of others, even if that largesse is dependent upon your efforts?

Disappointment anchoring her bare feet to the room she'd been allotted, she returned to the dreaded cot for however many more interminable hours remained until sunrise. But even wrapping her head in the blankets couldn't stop the quiet *thump* when the door closed.

With Mr. Chapman on the *other* side of it.

———◦∞◦———

A FEW MOMENTS PRIOR...

AFTER HE'D PACIFIED his belly and bladder and propped the back door open to allow a restless Barnabas out for a bit, Brier lounged half in/half out, waiting for his feline to return—and with the requested *dead* mouse. Or remains thereof.

"I'm not particular," he'd told the disappearing cat.

Now that it had finally stopped sleeting, though bone-chillingly cold, the brisk air felt invigorating to his un-jacketed form. The pinch to his lungs had nothing to do with the woman sleeping a few feet away, and everything to do with the frigid temperatures.

Keep telling yourself that, mate.

He would. Until he believed it.

An odd thump-scraping noise had him venturing a few feet beyond the shop, staring into the dim night now that his eyes had adjusted enough to see. But the sight of another tradesman—trades*woman*—dragging a heavy crate his direction, caused his chest to pinch for an entirely different reason.

For she was a female he recognized, despite their environs. One who should not be out this late. "Mrs. Hurwell!" he called, his legs making fast work of the distance remaining between them. What was his neighbor doing in the alley behind the shops? "How may I assist?"

"Mr. Chapman. How wondrous...to see you at this hour." She was woefully out of breath, back bent, arms outstretched so that her gloved hands grasped the ropes tied around the wooden rectangle. "You will be my...salvation tonight."

Why was her blight of a husband not lugging this burden?

Mr. Hurwell, the proprietor of *The Time Piece*, a clock shop and watch repair service of sorts located a few stores beyond, had an unhealthy predilection for gambling on horse races—if his trite equine-focused conversations were to judge by.

Brier was all-too-happy to avoid the some-what older, oft obsequious man when he could. His wife, now? Younger than Brier by a number of years, Hurwell's missus was vastly more pleasant than the codger she'd married. But why was she out unescorted?

"Here, let me." He took possession of the nearest corners and heaved. How had she made it this far on her own? "Your destination?"

"Chapman's ," she said with a slight grunt, turning to push her hip into it as he hauled. The diminutive Mrs. Hurwell, with her wealth of midnight hair and softly attractive bearing, was a pure waste on the old man her father had bound her to. Brier made it a point to check on her when he knew Hurwell was out of town, but he'd had no such knowledge this week. "Is Mr. Hurwell away from London? Traveling to see family?"

And without you? he wanted to shout but bit back out of respect.

"Nay." He took the ropes she'd been tugging by and pulled them loose so she could slip her scantly gloved hands free. Slowly reclaiming her breath, she straightened with a smile and pointed. "Yours, I believe. The crate. Delivered to our door by mistake. My husband is gone from home this eve, and not knowing what might be inside, I did not want your goods to wait."

"Thank you, but there was no need. A simple note or visit would have had me assisting you in a trice. And it certainly could have waited until tomorrow."

"Doubtful. It was left outside, along with one of ours. Any longer and footpads would have surely helped themselves. Only the weather kept it safe this long, I am sure." She glanced behind her at the alley she'd traversed, looking back at him with a bit of dismay—as though only now realizing what sort of danger she'd put herself in. "It isn't horridly far, and truth be told, I did not mind getting out." She mashed her lips together as though guilt loomed for offering such. "I confess, being cooped up in the shop without respite can be rather trying. But enough of that. I saw your new display—the horses and carriage are sparkish fine indeed."

He nodded, accepting the rare compliment for his efforts. "You must not have been by the front today, then?"

A brief shake of her heart-shaped face above a plain brown scarf wrapped tightly against the elements said she had not. "Did it sell?"

"Nothing so grand. Barnabas decided he wanted more room in the window."

"Oh no!" She gave a light, rueful laugh, clasping her hands in front of her scarf. "Nay, tell me he did not."

"He very well did. With verve and vigor. Toppled my hard-earned display straight onto the floor into a smashing array of broken pieces."

With verve and passion.

The words, so recently spoken and savored, echoed in his mind. Brought forth an image of the particular female who had consumed his thoughts the last day.

"Naughty of him," Mrs. Hurwell commiserated before brightening. "Sir Barnabas. Did I tell you—he brought me two mice and a beetle last week."

Brier chuckled, his ungloved fingers rubbing idly over the ropes he still held, damp and chilled and rough against his fingers. How had hers fared against the prickly twine, with naught but thin gloves that looked threadbare and lacking? A vision of other hands, newly bandaged, and so recently injured, filled his senses, beckoning him back to his abode, even as he focused on the female before him. "Aha. Now I know why he's been rumbling about at home, then. Giving you all of his best hunting efforts, he is."

With verve and passion...

"Mrs. Hurwell. I have a..." How did he describe her? His Fascination of the divine scent and delightful humor. "A visitor, at the moment. A female guest." *You sound as though you have just announced to the respectable Mrs. Hurwell you have a tart living under your roof.* "A-a genteel woman whose traveling trunk"—there! Tarts didn't travel with trunks, at least not that he knew of—"was destroyed when her carriage"—he applauded himself for remembering not to say *coach*—"was involved in an accident. There hasn't been time yet to have anything sewn up for her. Might you have a single day dress she could borrow? Or I could purchase from you? Aye, that would be better. You are much the same size. Anything would work, your oldest frock perhaps. It need not be elegant or of highest quality."

"Elegant," she all but snorted, gesturing to the outdated, voluminous coat cloaking her form. "You need not worry about that. Of a certainty, I will be happy to provide something. And there is no need to pay me for it. Let me return home and gather—"

"Oh no you don't." Dropping the ropes, he placed two fingers upon her forearm with only enough pressure to be felt past the heavy men's coat—likely pilfered from her scrub of a husband. "You will not be returning anywhere by your lonesome. Let me accompany you back to your abode"—like most others along their street, she and her mister resided above their shop —"and I shall count myself fortunate to be granted whatever dress you may spare. No matter *your* comfort in traversing such, I could not live with myself if I allowed a female to embark upon these alleys alone."

Yet you were ready to cast out not-loose Lucinda?

And that truth had him cringing inside as he checked his pocket for the key and knocked aside the brick holding the door open to allow it to shut securely before he escorted his companion home.

———⟫◦⟪———

"Mr. Chapman?" Lucinda couldn't halt the relief that coated her words and coasted over her heart the moment he unlocked and nudged open the back door. He'd been gone an age.

Upon hearing his approach—or perhaps only sensing it—she'd soared toward the door, hesitant feet be damned. The second she knew it was Mr. Chapman who ventured inside, she revealed herself. He'd left two candles burning in the narrow hall—one lit in a sconce along the wall, the other on a small table beside the door— allowing her to see the fatigue lining his hard-jawed face; dark hair, mussed and spattered with rain; and a fresh scratch along one side of his nose.

"Luce! What are you doing up?" He looked

stunning to her as he rose from anchoring the door wide with a brick or two. "Please tell me I did not wake you."

"You didn't. I could not sleep." He placed a paper-wrapped bundle just inside and then angled back out for a heavier load. "Here, let me help."

Together, they lugged a large crate over the threshold, but only after tipping it onto its narrow side, and shoved it up against the empty wall.

"Blazes," he exhaled, not quite out of breath. "Normally I would have left that outside and opened it there, not risked bringing inside any mice or other vermin that may have embedded themselves in the straw padding, but not at this time of night."

"You have been gone a rather long time." She worked to sound curious, not accusatory. "And heavens, where is your coat?"

He turned back from bolting the door and gave her an assessing look. "You heard me leave? How long have you been awake?"

"I have not yet slumbered. Not for a moment. Not since..." Did she say it? Did she bring it out into the open? "I have thought of nothing else save your lips since you titillated me with the promise of a kiss, Mr. Chapman."

"A promise, did I?" He wiped one forearm across his damp brow. "Please, not-loose Luce,

Mr. Chapman is for children and neighbors and considerate customers who do not simply herald me with a snap of their fingers. I would have you address me as Brier, if you would."

A fierce sort of pleasure took hold of her, for had she not heard the female voice identify him as *Mr. Chapman*?

"No coat, for I did not expect to be gone but a moment. And my neighbor pressed this upon me." He indicated the scarf snugged around his neck and shoulders, liberally speckled with scattered drips.

Avoiding calling him anything altogether—for *Brier* seemed so very intimate—she observed, "The drizzle has halted finally?"

"It is no longer coming down, only trickling from the eaves as the temperatures cannot make up their mind whether to freeze again or not." He unwound the scarf and draped it across the crate.

She stepped forward and brushed her fingers through his thick hair, dislodging several stray droplets. "Aye, the eaves caught up with you here."

And he caught her up to him, with strong arms around her waist, the chill of his fingers seeping straight through the borrowed nightshirt.

"Eek!" Stars and stockings, how strange and welcome his secure hold felt around her. How very odd yet alluring to have his muscular front against her softer one. The never-ending scents of the city under deluge—the rain dirtied by fumes and smoke, the soot and grime lining so much of the alleys—couldn't begin to overtake his personal fragrance, the one that drew her to him like the sun did blossoms.

"A kiss, you say?" His eyes glimmered as he shifted his hands, cold fingers digging in just above her waist. "It is in the offing, and not a yelp afterward?"

Her spirit soared, her cheeks spread in a smile, and even the soreness on one side couldn't stop her saucy words. "That depends on the quality of said kiss." She placed her hands over his, wishing she could feel his flesh past the bandages, gaining courage from the growing heat in his eyes. "A pitiful one might earn you a yelp— if one is warranted, that is."

"Whoa-ho! A minx I have before me now."

Her lashes fluttered downward. Her smile gentled even as her blood roared and heart thundered. "Never before have I been called such, thought of even. Nay"—she opened her gaze and sought his—"a sober miss of advanced years who associates with elderly pinchpennies does not necessarily a minx make."

He slid one hand from beneath hers to stroke his fingertips over her bruised cheek. "Ah, but a fearsome wench who braves beastly chases and strokes unworthy felines can seduce old widowers with ease."

"You are most assuredly not old."

"Tell that to my knees after stocking merchandise."

"What happened to your nose?"

"That unworthy feline."

Her throat made a noise of sympathy as her entire body began to shake. *You are really going to ask him? Now?* "Your deceased wife," she braved. "You have mentioned her several times." The clock in the shop began to chime midnight, slow ringing beats that echoed her quaking heart. "I take it the two of you loved well?"

His arms drifted away from her and he took a step back. Leaned his back against the wall. Still appearing fatigued, perhaps even more so.

Drat her tongue. "Forgive me, I should not have broached so personal a topic." Especially on Christmas, which it was, the chimes having ended.

"It is good you did. For I would not have secrets or questions between us. Not now that..."

"Now that?" she prompted when he remained silent.

He caught her gaze with his, then closed his eyes and banged the back of his head into the wall with a slight *thump*. Then again. "Not now that I find myself thinking of you far more than any other female of my acquaintance."

His eyelids flew open, head straightened from its assault. "As to my wife." His Adam's apple bobbed when he swallowed. "Alice and I loved hard and well." He brought one fist up to his chest and his dark eyes gleamed with remnants of grief. "Twice, she lost babes early in pregnancy. But after several years when we thought children were not in our future, she carried one to term, only to die along with our daughter at the birthing."

Luce reached toward his arm, only to yank hers back at the last second. Surprised when he snatched her wrist and held her hand between both of his as he finished. "Those were the darkest days I have ever endured, the months following her death, and that of our unnamed babe, who never even had a chance to draw breath."

His quiet, solemn voice rumbled its way between them. "As the years went by, I thought I was content to remain a bachelor. Had no use for women, other than as patrons with funds to buy my wares." His tired lips turned upward in a soft smile and he threaded his fingers through hers, brought the back of one hand up to his mouth, moved beyond the bandage until granting her wrist a brief yet devastating kiss, the quick swipe of his tongue reaching much farther than her arm.

"Until a venturous female with a penchant for stating her mind—even when she sounds the loon—somehow snared my interest without even trying." He gave her fingers a squeeze. "Though I loved Alice with everything in me, I have not loved—nor touched—another since.

And I find myself now craving that very thing. Fervently."

Blood rushed in her ears, her thoughts echoing all he said. All he had admitted. Had there ever been another man, so strong and so fine—and so very forthright?

"Yet you would like to...touch..." She pulled their joint hands to *her* lips, placing a soft kiss upon the back of his hand. "Touch *me* now?"

His gaze turned sultry. "More than anything," he rasped, stealing her breath. And if she were honest with herself, as the hitch in her chest confirmed, much more than that.

THEY WERE GOING to keep her! Merry, mewy Christmas!

Sheer delight rippled the fur down Barnabas's spine every bit as much as if he'd been treated to a luxuriant finger rub.

He jumped onto the wooden crate—after it passed his olfactory investigation, nose and whiskers working heartily around the base and up the sides, paying particular attention to the ropes. Mrs. Dorothea Hurwell, he could sniff out her scent—along with his man's—easily. The lovely neighbor gave good tail rubs, but more importantly she bestowed bits and bites of chicken and pork—when her skinflint of a sour man wasn't around.

Barnabas sunk his claws into the ropes with glee while giving the embracing couple surreptitious glances—no sense staring outright and making them uncomfortable or anything, not when he was getting exactly what he'd wished for.

7

A CURIOUS EVENING CALL

———◄○►———

WOULD SHE NOTICE HIS TREMBLING?

Brier straightened from the wall and gripped her upper arms. Had his belly ever fluttered at the idea of a simple kiss? Nay, for when he'd been younger, his untried prick stiffened anytime Alice came near, too impatient to know the bounty to be found in waiting, anticipating.

Now, though? His prick was primed all right, but the rest of him was just as eager. Just as raw.

He released one arm to trail a finger down the rainbow discoloring her cheek and jaw. "Does it ache?"

The swelling was obvious. The hues had leached toward one side of her mouth. Would it hurt her if he took her lips as hard as he desired?

"N-not when you touch me like that." A tremulous smile accompanied her words and she nuzzled into his fingers until his palm cupped her jaw.

In the cramped hallway of CHAPMAN's, near the back door leading to the alley, the space lit only by a couple withering candles, he drew her as close as he dared. Approached her bruised mouth with care, placed his lips upon hers and nibbled. Applied tiny kisses and lingering suction first to the bow of her upper lip and then to the plump one below. She wiggled within his embrace and his fingers drew downward from her face, wrapped around her torso and splayed across her upper back, pulling her against him.

A gentle, teasing flick of her tongue riled him faster than would have a blatant grope of his prick, the tantalizing swipe encouraging him to venture past her lips and kiss her without restraint.

Steady now, he cautioned himself. *Do not frighten her off.*

Frighten? Are you insane, man? Do you not feel the decadent scratches of her fingertips braving through your damp hair, gripping your scalp?

His answering moan confirmed he felt every nuance of her untutored, enthusiastic response. Every tentative foray of her tongue, meeting his —her excitement, matching his.

In moments, he was drowning, in over his head as passion engulfed caution, his arms pulling her tight against his chest, experiencing the twin mounds of her breasts plumped against his harder frame, her fervor equaling his as she opened her mouth and his tongue followed hers, their lips pressed tight together as they tasted and explored.

Who would have expected the first female to draw his eye in nearly a decade would prove combustible to his control? His impromptu visitor shredded it, of a certainty, given how his hands had started to roam. How the rest of him wanted to revel with her. *In* her.

Too soon, his hips tilted, ready to grind his erection into her stomach—or better yet, lower, against the apex of her thighs. When her hips slanted, meeting his ill-mannered lurch, a blast of sensation rode up his cock and settled, heavily, in his loins. Again, he pressed into her, kissed her harder, taking the alluring flavor of her into his mouth, breathing her in, as her low moan met his ears.

The soft but ragged sound somehow bellowing some sense into his brain.

He was the one with experience. The one responsible for what came next—and it wasn't going to be *him*, not inside of her. Not yet. Not this soon, no matter how much his blade and ballocks craved it. Craved her and the release she offered.

Because he wanted more than just a sensual Christmas Eve to remember.

He was starting to think he wanted it all.

LUCINDA COULDN'T CATCH her breath.

No matter. Who needed to breathe when life had given them such a boon? Her arms wrapped over his shoulders, crossed at the wrists, fingers delving through his thick hair and holding on. Keeping her steady as he plundered her mouth, stroked her tongue with his in such a way her abdomen angled toward him, found the hard ridge she'd not experienced before—

And found herself unable to stop rubbing against him.

Rubbing her fingers along his head. Her breasts, against his chest. Her tongue against his, within his mouth. Her most private, feminine self up and over, down and against, riding the firm pressure his body provided.

Had anything ever felt so good? So necessary?

Certainly, touching herself furtively beneath the covers, with the candles out and aloneness her solitary companion, had never—ever—felt so compelling, so—

Oh, you brazen tartlet, you—ruining your reputation on a whim?

She moaned, pushing away the intrusive voice, kissing him more fiercely, unwilling to relinquish—

"Luce. Lucinda," he murmured against her mouth, the loss of his tongue a painful ache. "Lucinda, we need to stop."

But his mouth retreated no farther, only gentled against hers, softened, pecked upon her quivering lips as his loins—and the rest of him—eased away, abandoned her needy self despite the whimper she couldn't hold back.

"I know," he said in a rasp meant to soothe, she was sure, though it did quite the opposite. "I know."

His broad palms braced against her shoulders—intent on keeping them apart? His forehead rested against hers, lips withdrawing as well—and she wanted to cry. To yell that she wasn't finished with him yet.

Her pelvis felt liquid and heavy, hollow without the press of him; her limbs pliable, as though the thick syrup of seduction ran through her instead of blood. And the insistent ache his body had roused grew stronger.

"I know, I do not want to halt either." His lips lifted to her forehead, kissed, and made their way to her temple, the whispered words tickling her ear and causing her stomach to clench. "You make me forget myself."

You make me find myself.

"'Tis after midnight."

"Happy Christmas," she said, gulping down sorrow and regret, fearful she might never again know anything as wondrous as the last few minutes.

"Think you can sleep?" he asked, his tone a soft husk.

"Not a wink."

"Mewrowll?"

"See there?" His lips breathed over the shell of her ear, fingers flexing on her shoulders as though maintaining distance strained him as much as it devastated her. "Barnabas is worried about you. Says he'll tuck you in, and the three of us can have a quiet Christmas tomorrow." When the store would be closed.

A mere two days before she made the outrageous Sunday call to secure a job. For a position she didn't want but desperately needed.

I need Brier more. What he makes me feel... remember. Family and laughter.

What he makes me yearn for...

The culmination of these heated kisses.

She wanted to sulk. Wanted to cry and tantrum. Her loins wept with wicked intensity. The peaks of her breasts called out for his hands. Her lips for his mouth.

Quivering, she licked hers. "Christmas." She'd given the holiday so little thought this year, so many other things battling for resolution. "I don't have you a gift."

And stop thinking of gifting him yourself.

He chuckled. Laughed outright, finally straightened and took one full step back, his hands sliding down her arms and then away. Leaving her alone. Barren. Save for the half grin he graced her with in the near dark, the closest candle having sputtered, a single waft of smoke its dying *goodbye.*

"Considering yon goodnight kiss is mayhap

the finest in memory, what other manner of gift could I have need of?"

———————◦◦———————

Ho, tomling! Are you near?

Was he being hailed?

Barnabas left off his kneading of the lightly "purring" female. For one who had been all topsy-turvy earlier this eve, after meshing mouths with his man (who had *never* laughed nor smiled so much as he had since their brief acquaintance began), she had fallen quickly to slumber after Mr. Chapman gifted her with clothing shared by Mrs. Hurwell.

Exclamations all around, surprise and appreciation most robust (even another kiss or four), until his landlord's slow steps retreated upstairs and their female changed into the feminine night-rail, sighed and drowsed off in a trice, soft murmurs and low whimpers accompanying her fitful doze. His attentions seemed to soothe, and what was he, if not generously accommodating? So he flexed and retracted, applied his paws against her restless form until—

Tomling! Kitty! I bid you come near.

Fish heads and turkey gizzards, he *was* being called!

Barnabas jumped from the cot, ducked beneath the curtain and raced toward the bow window, easily launching himself onto its spacious environs to stare out into the darkened night beyond.

The orange glow of beastly, if familiar, eyes his reward, fairly beaming from across the rain-slicked street. *There you are. Good. Is your female visitor still in habitance?*

Barnabas gave a single, slow-lidded blink.

Very well. I am relieved it is so. The man—being?—lifted a traveling bag. *I believe we located some of her belongings.*

The bolted front door drew Barnabas's gaze.

Nay. For it was locked when I tried. The alley? If I tuck it away back there, behind your shop, can you sniff it out, see it makes its way back to her?

"Mew."

———◦◦———

LUCINDA WOULD HAVE EXPECTED the harsh morning-lit hours following her first experience with clandestine, midnight kisses to be fraught with awkward hesitancy and uncomfortable moments. To her surprise, 'twas nothing of the sort.

Brier greeted her with a twine-tied, paper-wrapped package containing winter gloves for her healing hands, made of supple leather and fur lined; lengths of fabric—ones she'd admired when she hadn't realized he paid attention—sufficient to make up three day dresses; and most surprising of all, walking boots! Smashing-fine leather boots with a tiny raised heel and laces that went all the way past her ankles.

Muddling through her astonishment, she'd hugged her thanks, the appreciation quickly turning to more stirring kisses. Stepping back—eager to try on the new boots, thanks to the stockings gifted by the neighbor, Mrs. Hurwell—Luce bit her lips against the instinctive retort prompting her to rail at him for providing such a bounty.

What? Does he think you will now be his kept paramour? some guilty part of her chastised.

While another, wicked part, rejoiced at the chance.

"For shame," she finally said, losing her battle against the smile that curved lips and cheeks not quite as sore this morning. "For a stranger who had nothing to call her own mere hours ago, I have been indulged mightily."

And what was she ever going to give him? How could she ever repay him for the safety and security—the kisses she couldn't imagine doing without? How could she ever seek lonely employment outside of this haven he'd provided, the most agreeable accommodations she'd been blessed with since becoming an adult?

"I do not feel *stranger* embodies what we are to each other, Luce," he rumbled, all manner of heat brimming in his gaze, even as a light flush came upon his cheeks. "I am gratified you like what I managed to pull together."

"Like?" She had trouble not squealing her joy. Holding up one of the boots between them, she gave it a light shake. "I love. Adore. Cannot fathom how you accomplished so much so quickly."

The flush faded from his countenance, pride taking its place. "The gloves, I keep behind the counter, for patrons who inquire. The fabric, not-loose Luce..."

A gusty sigh escaped the mouth she couldn't stop staring at. He had yet to shave this day, dark bristle above his lips and coating his jaw tempting her to explore him all over again. Last night's kisses, even the few earlier this morning, seemed so very far away. "If you could have but seen the look upon your face when you chanced across those fabrics? 'Twas apparent they were meant to be yours, to swathe your frame, be fit and bound to lovingly grasp your form—" He coughed behind a fisted hand—as though the unexpected composition of his words surprised him as much as her.

He flicked the boot with one finger and sent it gently swinging within her grasp. "As to these? Consider yourself fortunate, indeed. For they were ordered—requested—by one of my sisters in her last letter, made and sized according to the drawing she sent. If they do not fit as you wish, we shall have others made up for you in a trice."

Her heart fell to her stomach, her stomach to the floor. The boot now hung listlessly by its laces, tight around her fingers. "I cannot take something meant for another. How can I ever repay you? You have done so much."

"I do not seek your money, nor repayment. Giving you these things elevates my spirits more than I would have fathomed mere days ago. That is all I need. As to my sister? It is a small matter to have another pair made for her—assuming these fit your feet as I hope they will."

The laces strangled a little less. "It is no small matter for me. None of your kindnesses are." She forced her gaze from his inviting mouth, from the endearing look he gave her. Then, resolution firming her tone, she announced, "I shall pay you back, reimburse you for all you have done. If not this companion job, then another I shall find. Or...or..."

"Lucinda. Stop." He untangled the ties from her fingers and dropped the boot, taking her hands in his and giving a warm and solid clasp to both. "Hear me well. Is Christmas not the season of giving? Of pleasure and family? You are here with me now, while mine is not. I ask nothing more from you. Not cleaning, certainly not kisses if they are given *in exchange*—"

"They have not been. Only given out of *want*." Of yearning. Of hope.

"And these things?" He knelt, retrieved the fallen boot and its mate, the strewn paper and loose twine, along with the fabrics and gloves she'd set aside. Rising, he pushed the neat bundle toward her middle until she had no choice but to grasp it. "They were given out of *want* as well. Nothing more than that. Certainly not out of expectation, of debt. Selfishly though, I gave you things because *I* wanted to be the one to bring you joy."

8

BRIARS, THORNS AND OTHER SHARPS

———⟨◦⟩———

"ENLIGHTEN ME ABOUT YOUR SIBLINGS? You have mentioned sisters."

The question shouldn't have surprised Brier, but it did, coming as it did during the first lull of silence between them. Since sitting down—actually, standing—across from each other at the long service counter to consume the bulk of the food remaining in his abode mid-afternoon.

The foodstuffs he'd tucked away last evening, when he realized how ill-prepared he was to entertain—and had not once considered replenishing supplies when he should have, all of his attention the last two days focused either on his prime visitor or upon those annoying mistakes in the account journals.

Accounts? he could practically hear his older brother Sharpe guffawing. *That's what you claim owns half your attention today? If Mama heard that bounder, she'd wallop you but good.*

Shoving aside the astute assessment, he studied his delightful Christmas companion.

Talk had flowed between them like a river, twisting and turning, soaring over rocks, abutting into banks, their blather flitting from topic to topic, lightly and laughingly—until her unexpected question dammed up that river faster than a quake, recalling to mind everything she'd shared the day before.

The misfortunes she'd endured far more serious than the more inconsequential topics they had touched upon while consuming a stew of chicken and vegetables, particular to each of their personal likes and dislikes: literature, composers, instruments, favored Bible verses, affinity for seasons, sites in and beyond London... They had conversed with ease upon it all.

And now they were to delve further into *families*? Exceeding the tragedies she had already confided?

"'Tis a pathetic selection, eh?" He nudged the half-eaten boiled cabbage he'd thought to add at the last minute with his fork, gaining time, deciding how best to proceed. Then released it to place his second slice of bread—untouched, but at least buttered and toasted—upon her dwindling plate. "Eat that too. My stores are so meager, I should be contrite"—he grinned at her, taking up the utensil to scoop a substantial bite of carrots and potato—"for not serving you a more exalted holiday meal, but I confess, this tastes better than it should, thanks to the company, I am sure." He toasted her with his fork before the contents disappeared down his gullet.

Hoped she didn't notice him mincing his chicken and sneaking more than he should have to the feline who kept twining around ankles and leaning against calves.

"Never have I enjoyed a Christmas more," he told her honestly, near stunned at the realization. To think, he would have spent the day just like any other, alone and task-busy, before she arrived and topsy-turvied his plans. And his life.

"Nor I." She severed the bread and placed the larger half back on his plate. "We shall indulge equally."

"And I shall procure more of a selection tomorrow." Tomorrow, when she would leave to procure a job, unless he could find a way to convince her otherwise. His appetite gone, he nudged his plate aside.

"They were not figments, were they?" she prompted with a smile at his continued silence.

Brier cast off his slow-to-depart uncertainty— or at least attempted to. "My sisters? I do indeed possess a fine pair. Along with a trio of brothers, that no one in their right mind would describe as *fine*."

"Both a pair and a trio? My, you must have led your parents a merry dance."

"I... Hesitate to regale you with tales of...our frolics when you— When..."

"Given my lack? You waver because of my lack of family, of siblings?"

He knew she had come from a small family, one destroyed when her older sister first went missing, and then, devastatingly, turned up dead two years later—or so they assumed, the female's body having the same color of hair and being close to the anticipated size, but being weathered, leading the authorities to conclude it was her, but without absolute certainty. Hinting little at her own grief and sacrifices, Luce had shared about the years spent caring first for her father, and then her mother, as both mourned themselves to death, and Luce having no other close family.

Though he tried to keep it stifled, he suspected every bit of sadness he felt on her behalf showed in his expression. "After what you have endured," he said now, "the brave way you have handled the staggering loss of your family, how can I expound upon my bounty? Trouble-some though they can be at times. *Most* times," he added, hoping to see her smile.

And was rewarded with that and with the gentle touch of her fingers trailing over his hand —now clenched, he saw, white-knuckled around his fork. "You can," she said as light as her touch, "because I would never begrudge another's happiness. Especially not you. Come now. Expound away."

Especially not him?

Dare he take that to mean some part of her was starting to see him in a fond light, perhaps something even akin to how he had so quickly begun viewing her?

Much more familiarly—fervently—than fondly, eh?

"All right. But I give you leave to bid me stop at any time. There are a host of us, spanning seventeen years. Two brothers, not much older, Thorne and Sharpe. One brother, younger than myself—Clayton. And the two sisters you will recall me mentioning, Rose and—"

"Stop!" Laughing, she sank her teeth into her bottom lip to curtail the sound he hadn't expected. "Stop now, you knave. For I know you jest me most cruelly. You, *Brier*, and now you claim *Rose* and *Sharp*"—more laughter—"a-and *Thorn*? Oh, please! Next you will be alleging Dirt and D-Daisy." She nearly choked. "How you expect me to believe anything..."

He was delighted at her mirth. Cared not it was at his family's expense. For they *were* quite nonsensical, the lot of them, their names the least of it. "Can I help it if Mama had Papa reading *All's Well That Ends Well* as her lying-in approached? That she latched on to Helena's scene-ending speech?"

"Not having every Shakespearean scene-ending speech commended to memory, commoner that I am, can you elucidate?"

"You are not common. Did we not already establish that?"

"You are not old."

"Hurrumph." She'd repeated that refrain a time or ten, chiding him if he dared refer to himself as anything but young and spry—and he had to admit, being with her, yearning for her as a man twenty years his junior, made him feel significantly younger than he had of late. Made him think as though it wasn't too late to latch on to something himself.

So perhaps, he would show her...

"Let me rectify."

HER BODY-SHAKING GIGGLES FINALLY SUBSIDING, Lucinda nibbled at the bread she'd shared. How absurd of her to think it romantic that they each partook of a portion of the same slice.

Castle-spinning ninny.

"Elucidation shall be yours, my uncommon lovely." With that, he pushed away from the counter and came around so she could see him fully. He bent his knees, bowed his back and propped one fist on a cocked hip as though mimicking every aged matron he'd ever seen.

She swallowed quickly, lest she choke, knowing he was about to entertain her with one of his humorous bits—as she suspected his entire "sibling" response had been. (Simply to entertain, to bring a laugh to her lips and a lightness to her heart. Ridiculous man—did he not know that simply being near him had begun to do that without any effort at all?)

Affecting a high, feminine pitch and speaking as though he was sorely aggrieved, he quoted (and *toddled*)...

> "The time will bring on
> *summer*,
> When *briers* shall have
> leaves as well as *thorns*,
> And be as sweet as *sharp*.
> We must away, *dear*
> maiden;
> To sleep, to *slumber*, to
> snuggle
> All's well that ends well;
> Goodnight."

When he finished mimicking the majestic words of the Bard, she was laughing so hard tears leaked from the edges of her eyes. "You rotten scoundrel! That cannot be how the lines went. 'To sleep, to slumber'?"

"To *snuggle*, lest you forget." He stood tall and returned to his normal, bracing voice. "And aye, I modified the ending, but not the beginning. I vow to thee."

"Vow to thee?" She giggled again. "You, Brier *Bamming* Chapman, brother to none—mayhap one—son to a patiently revered saint, I am sure, will be smote if you keep trying to bamboozle me."

"You believe me not?" As though he trotted across the stage every night since first growing fuzz upon his face, he brought both hands to his chest and jerked back in the manner of one suffering a killing blow. "You wound me, my fair maiden. Wound me mightily." He crumpled to the floor as though the tiny hit to his pride had been monstrous indeed. "For I have been smitten, by you. Can you not tell?"

Which only caused her mirth to magnify.

After he regained his feet and brushed off his seat, her smote-smitten companion of the farcical lines and nonsensical manner launched into outlandish descriptions of his "supposed" siblings.

"You will quickly see I remain the most humdrum of our crew," he began, but already Lucinda shook her head.

She pointed toward the area of his recent performance. "*Humdrum,* you are certainly not."

"Let me see. Closest to me in age there's Sharpe, always with an E."

She waved her hands in the air. "Do not tell me. I must guess. Sharpe is a master swordsman? A fencing expert?"

"Ah, nothing quite so assumable. Nay, he's more of a sharper at the card table."

"A swindler?" she asked leaning forward,

curiosity overtaking skepticism for a moment. "Never have I met a defrauder."

The skin between his eyebrows pinched. "You need not sound so enthralled over the prospect."

She bit back more of a smile at the hint of his pout. "Rather a bit of competition between the two of you, I take it?"

"Rather the gouger practiced his skills on unsuspecting siblings, rendering one of them"— he aimed a finger toward his chest—"completely without funds one entire year at school."

"That, I can sympathize with. No funds is certainly no fun." Both of them chuckled when her words came out thus. "Who else?" she inquired.

"Thorne, also with an E, fancies himself something of a pirate."

"A *pirate*?" Silent laughter puffed her cheeks and rolled her eyes. As if she would fall prey to such a claim.

"Aye. Even though he's an earl."

She snorted out loud at that. "An earl? Oh-ho!" If she had harbored even a modicum of doubt before, it was gone now, banished by his absurdity. "Why not make your pirate brother a duke?"

"Oh, Thorne would like that." He nodded, as though consigning to memory to tell said "fabricated" brother. "One sister is Rose. She's a perfumist."

"Perfumist? I doubt that's a word." Luce

dusted her fingers off and snuck an impatient Barnabas the remaining morsels of her chicken —for the other scoundrel in residence had just applied teeth to her calf.

"It is, most assuredly."

But the mischievous grin that played with his lips again made her doubt. "I do not know whether I shall believe you."

"'Tis your choice. Would you prefer...ah, *perfumery expert*?" He snapped his fingers. "Fra-grancearian!" Declared with a remarkably serious expression—totally belied by the humor lighting his eyes.

As if she'd believe *anything* he told her about his family henceforth. "*Mmm-hmm* Any others?"

"Of my imaginary siblings? The ones you believe inhabit my idea pot instead of the grounds of England?"

"Aye, those."

Really, his talent for farce was lost in the mercantile. Her rescuer, Brier (with an E)—he of the demanding kitty, strong arms and heated kisses—had missed his theatrical calling.

"There's Eve."

"Eve? Not Pinprick? Or Pointe, *with an E*, of course."

"Luce. Your mistrust is like one of Sharpe's phantom swords to the heart."

She rubbed her ear and gave him a doleful look beneath her lashes. "All right. *Eve.* Born on the eve of Christmas, no doubt."

"Nay."

"Midsummer's, then. From the play."

"Shakespeare's *A Midsummer Night's Dream*, you mean? No *eve* in sight. Tut-tut, Lucinda. Whoever was responsible for your literary education? Wrong again."

He bent to scoop up Barnabas, who draped over his master's shoulder as though he did it every day. "Nothing so predictable," he chided, scratching fingers over the cat's striped back. "By now, Mama had reached the end of her list of names. Fortunately Papa was reading aloud *Measure for Measure*. Named for 'All-hallond's' eve, she was. Better known as the evening before All Saints' Day."

"You would have me believe pretend *Eve* was named after Halloween?" Luce shoved at his closest (cat-free) shoulder. "You are core-rotten to jest so handily at my expense."

When she reached for his empty plate, he clapped one hand over her forearm and stayed her. "You do not want to hear about the rest?"

Her entire arm heated from his touch; belly clenched. Lips tingled. "How many more?"

"Clayton. He has an affinity—"

"Where's the E?"

"His second name. Clayton Elliot Jeremy Chapman."

"Of course. Pardon my interruption. Affinity for...?"

Barnabas squirmed and Brier plucked him off

his shoulder and let the cat slide to the floor. "Bugs. Insects," he said, rising. "He likes dirt—"

"Dirt! Did I not say you would profess a brother just so?"

Brier just gave her an indulgent grin. "His name is not *Dirt*; well...Clay. You may have me there. But truly, he is *enamored* with it and the nasties it teems with. He collects specimens—"

She gave a shudder—not quite feigned. "Who else?"

"Well, there are the triplets, Shakes and Spear and—"

"Now I *really* do not believe you! Not a word."

"They aren't exactly—"

"You fiend." She slid her hand free. "'Tis the sharper I have before me now."

"You shall see..."

"See what?"

"Whether I play you false—if you will agree to stay by my side, for all our Christmases to come."

———◦———

HAD HE REALLY SAID THAT?

Stay by my side for Christmases to come...

So soon?

Aye, I did. And I meant every syllable.

But Brier's timing had been deplorable.

With Luce's all-encompassing disbelief about his tag-rag family, she had taken his heartfelt avowal as naught but another jest, bustling from the counter, both their empty plates in hand, to step out the back and rinse them under the newly falling rain.

Putting an abrupt end to the moments of mirth.

But not to his determination.

9

A CHRISTMAS-WORTHY CUDDLE

———— ❧ ————

"Aha! A whisker." Lucinda smiled over her discovery, kneeling to pluck it from the floor, drawing Brier's gaze for what seemed the hundredth time the last hour. "How long has Barnabas been with you?"

She asked this from the ladies' display, where she had been rearranging sundries late that afternoon, during those few moments betwixt daylight and dark, when enough light near a window permitted work to carry on. Brier took more satisfaction than he had a right to, watching her flit about, touching his things.

No matter that the *things* in question were not personal to him. No matter that her guileless fingering of merchandise was not intended to seduce his senses and bungle his brain, it did so nevertheless.

Her efforts with the ribbons and small bit of garland he'd left for her, combined with her cut-out snowflakes, proved sublime, such that the Christmas spirit flowed from the store on into the back storage areas and up the staircase to his lodgings—where her labors had, understandably, halted. Not that he had locked her from his rooms nor forbade her entry. But what manner of self-respecting man encouraged a female into his domain?

Tension hunched his shoulders over the accounting journal he'd been studying since their midday repast. The distracted scrutiny had yet to resolve the remaining math errors plaguing the entries, thanks to that last, disastrous assistant. But his tension wasn't the fault of the books. More the fault of his ballocks. His blame, misbegotten yearnings to lock the doors—with her inside. *With him.*

"Did he find you or you him? Were you seeking a cat?"

The quiet hours of Christmas Day, with the shop closed, cold winds still blowing, keeping sleet and ice frozen up against the eaves and in the shadows, had scurried by swifter than Brier could ever remember. How many more would he be fortunate to count with his current companion? Before commitments and life ripped her from his? Tore her soothing, unexpectedly charming presence from a life he had not realized had become so very barren?

"Woo-hoo. Bri-*er*..." The rare use of his name, so very welcome upon her lips, pulled his attention back where it preferred to dwell—upon her. "Have you had him long?"

"Barnabas? The vagrant stole in one night. Promised he'd earn his keep in the warehouse, down near the dock, but instead lazes around on his duff, staring at me anytime I pull out a bowl or plate, expecting me to wait on him as though he were royalty."

Her lilting laugh dove straight to his middle, stirred up things better left settled. Especially if she remained intent on leaving once the weather cleared.

To stifle the urge to walk over to her, to take her in his arms and haul her upstairs, he cleared his throat. Clenched the innocent pencil in a death grip and offered, "Neither scolding nor shaming has convinced him to be a better mouser. He seems to think barely one small, shitten rodent a week is sufficient for bed and board."

"No wonder the idler has such an appetite. He shared nuncheon with me, I admit."

"You mean *you* shared with him?"

"Aye," she said with a winsome smile.

He'd seen how she'd carefully separated the meat from the bone—but hadn't realized she'd been slipping the little gangrel part of her meal— for he'd been doing the same. "That little roamer.

He knows how to gain indulgences from us both, I fear."

Missing the demanding rub of the feline around his ankles and calves, something he'd come to take for granted as evening approached and he stilled from his industrious bustle of the day, Brier straightened and pushed away from the counter. "Where is the lazy louse? Have you seen him recently?"

She left off aligning the attar bottles to scan their environs. "I have not, not since losing a good portion of my chicken to him."

"Mayhap I let him out and simply do not remember." It wasn't as though the account journal had occupied a significant portion of his thoughts since their meal. Nay, for those were completely focused on the female a few feet away.

Frustrated with his lack of concentration more than the erroneous entries, plagued by his own insistent desires of whisking her up and away, tucking her snug in his bed—and keeping her there—his restless fingers dropped the pencil and tapped against the accounts that consumed his attention.

Sure they do. Thorne's voice in his head this time

"You always brick the door," she said, walking the shop, checking the nooks and corners where he'd seen her pet his feline previously. "And then

you unbrick it when he comes in. You are scrupu-
lous in your actions, I have observed."

True. He kept it propped open, so the cat
could skulk back in as soon as he was ready and
locked it upon Barnabas's return. After a theft
two years ago, while one of his brothers minded
the shop during Brier's visit home, they'd
attached a chain on the door, and when engaged,
it wouldn't yield to a human body, only a
feline one.

She was back at the window, hand mirror
held before her visage. She lowered it, and made
a face at him. "If I was an actress, and knew how,
could I use cosmetics to hide the array, do you
suppose? What elderly female wants a green-
and-yellow-tinged companion?" Her eyes grew
big and she smiled. "Perhaps she will be just as
stingy as my last employer, allow candles only for
company, and as long as I keep this side to the
shadows, perhaps I have a chance at winning her
favor."

"You still fret over that?" He had half a mind
to find cosmetics and paint the bruise darker and
bigger—if it would only keep her here.

She approached and laid the mirror on the
counter. "No longer. Now I fret over Barnabas. I
shall look in the alley. Do you mind going
upstairs, checking your lodgings?"

Brier took hold of her wrist before she could
run off. "*You*, please, go upstairs and look for him.

I will peruse the alley. That is no place for a female alone."

The delicate muscles and sinew flexed within his grasp. "All right. Thank you. Does he have a favorite spot? Upstairs?"

"Curled atop the bed coverings. Sprawled near the hearth, just beyond the coal bin. Sometimes on the table—aye, where I eat." He started shaking his head, gave her wrist a gentle squeeze and then headed toward the back door before he could utter anything more embarrassing.

A grown man, letting his mouser lounge on his table? *Tut, tut.*

IT WAS SIMPLY A ROOM. A small gathering of spaces.

Nothing extravagant. Nothing to alter the core of her being, but upon ascending the stairs and braving Brier's private domain, a wave of acute homesickness rolled over Lucinda like the vast ocean inundating the shore.

For his lodgings, though modest, felt like *home*. Welcomed her inside and invited her to explore.

His scent imbued the space, slightly musky and wholly male. His presence evident everywhere she turned: a Bible on a small table next to his bed, covers rumpled, an empty circular space giving evidence where Barnabas had napped earlier. A pair of boots, another of shoes, lined up against the wall, beneath a row of pegs upon which three shirts and two pair of pants draped, hanging downward, ready for his hand to pluck them free and don them at the beginning of his next day.

The hearth he'd mentioned hailed her attention, the space disappointingly empty of feline. Above, along a mantle: a comb, a ring, a dried leaf and uniquely striped rock... The little things that created comfort out of space. Warmed the heart on cold nights.

"Barnabas? Come on out, sweet boy." Inhaling Brier's scent down to her toes, she knelt and lifted the fallen bedcovers. No kitty beneath. Nor snugged under them either. The square table across the room barren as well. "Come on, you stubborn cat. Where are you?" Luce circled the space, calling to no avail.

Drawn to Brier's one visible indulgence, she approached a giant mahogany and leather chair tucked away near the eaves on the opposite side of the room. The wooden arms and upper back decorated with intricate carvings; 'twas the sort of chair one found behind an affluent lord's desk, where he carried out his business and duties, not the sort one usually found stashed away above a mercantile.

A couple of pricks in the leather seat made her wonder if Barnabas liked to place his sharp claws where he shouldn't, but he wasn't there now.

She made her way behind the screen at the narrowest, farthest point from the entrance and found shaving paraphernalia next to a wash-basin, lit well by the pair of windows that looked out over the street. The chamber pot he kept tucked farther back, away from view of any passers-by and the shops across the road.

Confident no kitty lurked unspied and ready to return downstairs to learn whether Brier had better success, she slowly turned...eyes drifting languidly over every inch... Strangely reluctant to leave. Not when his presence imbued the very air.

Something out the window caught her attention. Across the way—seized it, as a barb did a loose garment or unprotected skin. Could it be the missing cat?

Night had deepened, clouds hovered over-head, giving the atmosphere outside an ominous feel. She bent closer to the window, strained to identify what had commanded her attention.

Only to see a familiar pair of wickedly glowing eyes.

Terror gripped, hard and fast, sunk its talons into her mind as her body instantly relived every horrifying second of the dreadful journey through the black night and sinister streets of London. Her feet aching, body numb from the cold, heart exhausted from furious pounding. Dashing pell-mell through the murk and the gloom of empty streets—save for the intimidating *whoops* of the threatening, if distant, canting crews and the ghastly glow of the eyes never far behind...

Irrational fear climbed up her throat and burst out as her feet abandoned earthly gravity and flew heavenward, hove above the steady floor with a speed that defied physics.

At the stairs, she heedlessly careened her body downward—to safety.

To—

"Brier!"

———◦◦———

Brier!

Down in the alley, partially veiled by the mishmash of offcasts surrounding him, the female's shriek, coming from his home above the shop, rang plainly in Barnabas's ears, the triangular, tuft-tipped tops of his furry self impressive indeed, both in function as well as form. The scars along the right one? Proof of his prowess among his peers. His superiority.

Nevertheless, the high-pitched scream rippled the fur down his back, causing him to wince at the discomfort.

Whatever could have caused such a screak of distress?

Mayhap she saw a mouse?

He barely avoided snickering, extending his claws and piercing the worn travel bag he'd sniffed out earlier. The one he'd pushed and prodded, kneaded and clawed, trying to drive the lumpy items to the outer edges and make a pleasant little nest for his worthy self.

But that shrill squall of hers? His ears still buzzed.

Mayhap he should rouse himself to do his man a boon and bring him a few more of the tailed rodents than he had provided of late?

He yawned, stretching one front leg out and dragging his claws forward, enjoying the slight sting as they caught on the thick, already fretted fabric.

Mayhap not. For he had more than earned his keep over the years, and now 'twas past time for his landlord to discover his sleek self guarding the parcel of goods delivered by Barnabas's new, mysterious friend.

Oh, but what pitiful timing on her part, to wail *now*, as his landlord had just spied those striking ears of his and *finally* approached...

———— ❧ ————

"B-R-I-E-R!"

The utter and complete screeched curdle of his name tore Brier away from his discovery. Whipped him around. Hied his feet back inside faster than a blink.

"Luce! What—"

She slammed into him. Knocked him back

two steps. Climbed up his body. Slung her arms tight over his shoulders, her hands digging through his hair, clutching at his scalp.

"Luce, what are you—"

"'Tis him!" she gasped, trying to burrow against his chest. "Eyes... Glowing..."

Her fear conveyed. Heart thundering, he held her. Gripped her. Soothed her frantic pants and disjointed mutterings until gaining understanding. Offered to go outside and confront—

"Nay," she pleaded, holding him ever so tightly. "Stay. Remain." *Keep me safe*, she begged.

How could he deny such a request? When in his arms was exactly where he wanted her?

A LONG WHILE LATER, the two of them ensconced within his favorite, oversized chair in Brier's private lodgings, her agitation had finally calmed, with time and his touches. With his assurances: he *would* keep her safe—a vow he took to heart. (Even if he had to pull out Sharpe's discarded dueling pistols to see it done.)

The hour had grown late, his unrepentant puss returned and now slumbering contentedly by the coal bin—heedless of the worry his little external jaunt had caused.

The room was dim, their voices hushed—when their mouths weren't occupied with things other than *talking*.

Luce nuzzled her head against Brier's jaw. Plucked at the open collar of his shirt, loosened thanks to her fingers and the "soothing" kisses he'd bestowed (ones that had much the opposite effect—on them both, he surmised).

"I looked at the accounting journal you had on the counter, when you went back outside, to snare Barnabas." Who had given him a sharp claw for his efforts.

She exhaled a long sigh, as though finally ready to release her earlier fear. "Not trying to overstep or insert myself into your business, mind, but I noticed two numbers that were transposed on the page you were studying. Another transposition, and a basic math error on the next."

"You did?" Relief sounded in his voice. "I have been scouring the last several weeks' entries for errors left by my last—inept—assistant, trying to make sense of the hubble-bubble he created.

"That was the last section not in my handwriting." Did Brier tell her he'd been studying the blasted page all day? That her presence had made it all but impossible to concentrate? "I located seven other errors to date, but you found three more?" His arms tightened around her. "Hallelujah. Between the two of us, we may just have discovered the remaining conundrum that was tying my noodle in knots.

"Show me later?" He breathed deep, enjoying

the presence of her weight in his lap. "I am vastly too content to move right now."

"I marked them with a small circle, to the left of the number. Something light that you could erase if you did not—"

"Nay. That is absolutely perfect. Thank you. Could I, perhaps, interest you in a job?"

"A job? As your assistant?" She chuckled, as though dismissing the notion out of hand. She left off playing with his shirt to curve her fingers around his neck until gripping his nape. "I know it's *terribly* brazen of me to ask..." she began in a whisper and then paused.

"Ask away."

"Would... Could we..."

At her continued dithering, he encouraged, "Speak freely, if you would. Have we not done so since meeting each other?"

"I confess, I am worn to a frazzle this eve. Likely became anxious over naught...a candle, mayhap? A lantern?" She shifted within his arms, pulled back to meet his eyes in the flickering candlelight of their own, hers looking boldly abashed, if that were possible. "But would it be... Feasible...in any way...for us— For you—" She ducked beneath his chin once more and finished in a rush. "For you to hold me tonight? While we sleep—*sleep*—together? But not, not do—"

"Not do anything more than *hold*?"

Her head bumped his chin when she jerked a nod.

"'Twould be my honor."

It also might be the death of him. Would he even sleep? Doubtful, the idea of keeping her close throughout the night hardening him like a metal rod, something he would disguise with plenty of blanket bulked between them.

Because he wouldn't abandon this opportunity, not for all the unbreakable white porcelain horses in the world.

CHRISTMAS IS COMING; OH, WAIT. IT ALREADY CAME!

A SLIGHT TENSING was his only warning.

"Know you're awake," Brier whispered against the wispy strands of Luce's hair, resting against his lips. He willed his prone body to remain as still as hers. "Please don't be afraid. Or scream. I won't—" *Try anything.* As though she would believe that. "Do anything *more.*"

Dawn approached unrelentingly...but wasn't here in full, not yet, all dark grey shadows beyond the windows. Would she spring from him now? See his treacherous, unconscious movements during sleep as reason to no longer trust?

Angst clutched at his heart for he wasn't ready to release the night, much less the female against him. The woman previously replete and slumberous within his embrace, now clenched head to chilled toes in the quiet of his abode.

No wind howling, no rain spattering, for the first time in what seemed an age. The winter storm had passed, then? Leaving him snuggled around the female in his arms.

In his bed.

Her back to his front.

Her innocence yielding to his illicit actions...

He started to retrieve his fingers from where they nested, splayed at the top of her pubic mound.

She gave a squeak and clasped his forearm.

Ack. Had his motion only just told her where his traitorous hand had ventured?

Beneath the bed coverings, his bare feet shifted, causing him to groan when he nudged one of hers. "It was there when I awoke. My hand."

As though curving his slumbering body around the warm female in his bed was the most natural thing in the world...despite the years since he had done so...

As though his mental yearnings had coalesced into physical actions, he had, during the night, rucked the hem of her night-rail and placed his open, relaxed hand upon her abdomen, sliding downward until the very tip of his middle finger rested in the hollow just above her pearl. The tiny nub he would give his right ballock to search out, to stroke...

But he had no right. No right to nudge his needy fingers along the warmth of her folds. His fingers—entire hand—now aching from holding so very still.

Without volition, his fingers twitched and he bit back a second groan at the warmth of her. "Was afraid to startle you if I moved it earlier."

"Please." It was a sighed breath of wonder, of awe. "Do not."

His, of a certainty. Awed at the invitation he heard.

He flexed his hand, amazed at how well the pad of his finger fit, nestled within that warm, welcoming hollow, his other fingertips spread and lightly grazing the softly crisp hairs guarding her entrance. "Don't...move?" He sought to confirm. "Are you positive?"

Her body strained against his in a long stretch though she kept her clasp firm upon his forearm, kept his fingers anchored. "I confess to wishing for just such a touch." Her words were as froth, airy in the predawn light surrounding his bed. "Or if not such a touch *exactly*"—the clutch on his arm eased and she reached for his hand, twining her fingers within his—"then something similar. Not having any...well, direct experience beyond that of my own."

At that, her fingers fluttered over his, as though emboldening them—him—to commence.

"Ah. An inexperienced virgin, then?" *And how could you ask thus? To a near stranger!* 'Twas quite easily done, given their proximity. Their ease with one another. Her encouraging dance over his hand, the unmistakable tilt of her pelvis.

Brier allowed his longest finger to travel. Back and forth, just a fraction. And then, with no verbal protest forthcoming—not that he expected any—up and down. *Down*, delving deeper toward her cleft and the warmth beckoning his touch secreted within.

"Quite the inexperienced virgin," she said lightly, "and me—at my ripe age."

"Right, because you are such a trot," he said in utter disbelief, as though anyone could consider the prime female inhabiting his bed an oldster. "So *very* ancient."

"And your feeble self? A whoremonger?" She snickered at the last word, as though even saying it surprised her.

"Aye. One of the greatest whoremongers of our time. I, who remained a virgin myself until I met my dear Alice, who remained faithful to her during our marriage, and—" *to her memory ever since.*

But that wasn't the truth. Not any longer.

Not given his imaginings of the last forty-eight hours. Had it truly been that brief of a time? For it seemed as though he had hungered for the woman in his arms now—for Lucinda—for an eternity.

It wasn't tarrying angst for his departed

beloved that had kept him from bringing another to his bed. It was practicals. And interest. Here in London, he didn't exactly move in the sort of circles where widows hopped freely from one bedchamber to another. The women who frequented his establishment, with intent to peruse and purchase, were the respectable sort. And the others who liked to barge and bang in, *not* the sort he had any interest in joining for a bang.

"Mr. Chapman. *Brier.*" She sighed the last, releasing his gently probing fingers and brought her arm up, curving her hand over the side of his face and around to his nape, where she gripped skin and scalp in a secure hold. "Never tell me, dear sir. Have you remained pure since becoming a widower?"

He barked an uncomfortable laugh. "When you put it thus, I sound an imbecile."

Her legs widened, encouraging farther journeys south, her upper foot finding his lower, pant-covered leg and starting to graze (making him wish he'd not portrayed such a gentleman in leaving them on overnight). "Not an imbecile. Never that. A decent man."

He'd found her button, that tiny nub his Alice had liked, had slicked and squealed when he caressed. And then he let her memory, the one he'd clung tight to in his grief and subsequent years, settle comfortably, calmly, in a portion of his heart that would always belong to her, even as that same portion—and all the rest—opened wide to allow for new memories. New love. For Lucinda.

Gathering her closer, he feathered his finger over that small area and the flesh around it, content, oh so content, at the feeling of a receptive, surprisingly enthusiastic woman in his arms once more.

"A decent man, you suppose? A man *famished*, more like." He could not help but growl as her fingertips started scratching gently through his hair. He nuzzled the lightly scented space behind her ear. "Famished for you, Luce, not for a memory, lest you wonder."

"I hadn't. But it's comforting to hear. Especially—" She gasped, arching into his touch. "When you persist in...doing such brazen things."

"Persist?" Her gliding flesh, the thrust of her loins against his hand—their joint and breathy eagerness—guided his longest finger past silken flesh until entering. "If my persistent touch is repellent, it could always retreat."

Her inner walls clutched tight. "Retreat and I will have Sharpe's sword at your throat. Clay's specimens on your dinner plate."

Chuckling, groaning, loving every moment they spent together, Brier coaxed a satisfyingly loud release from the now (somewhat) experienced virgin in his arms.

He rolled her over to face him and kissed her like a man possessed. Which he was.

◆━━━━●○●━━━━◆

"GREETINGS, LONDON BRO!"

"Yo-ho! Brier! Where are you, sleepyhead?"

"Be like him...stay open...midnight...hoping... business."

The unmistakable sounds of scrambling and laughter nudged his awareness, but the warm, replete bundle in his arms commanded his muzzy attention.

Until the next voice shouted, "Yo, Brier Edgar Isaac! We may be days late, thanks to the ice and dire state of the roadways, but we're here, you ingrate! Show yourself."

His warm bundle turned to cold stone the same instant Brier's slumberous mind made sense of the interruption. His arms tightened around Luce, as though to contain the private moment. "Blazes! That's Thorne. Didn't know he was back in England."

"Rouse from bed and join us!" the feminine voice of his youngest sister prodded. "We brought Christmas dinner to you."

"Half frozen by now," one of his brothers muttered.

From the sound of it, the rogues were already moving merchandise and displays and shoving tables together, likely burying his long counter with Christmas pudding, goose and other treats.

"Gracious me." Luce's head brushed his chin as she spoke. "They are *real*?"

"What? My family? Of course they are."

"I know you didn't go anywhere, Bri." The first voice again. "Refused to close up shop... Travel to visit..."

"No, they aren't," she protested. "For you made them all up to entertain—"

Brier rolled her over, until she was on her back and he could angle his torso over hers, nudge one of his legs decadently against hers as she stared up at him, disbelief writ all over her features. He cradled her face, palms on either side as he threaded his fingers through her dark locks—now in beautiful disarray and more inviting than ever after they'd heated water for washing before retiring last eve.

"Nay, Luce. Every word I have spoken to you is truth. *Every* one."

"And they are *here*?" she squeaked. "*Now*?"

"Regrettable timing, I know." What was this going to do *to them*? Him and Luce? To his chances of convincing her—

"Brier!"

"Come on, Bri!"

His siblings were coming closer.

Desperation twisting his belly, he yelled, "Who all is there?"

"Just the returned prodigal"—that was Clay,

referring to Thorne—"Eve and myself. Get your laze-about carcass down here."

"Rose is back with the ancients"—Thorne's voice grew louder—"wondering why your sorry arse didn't travel home before all this hit."

As though he could predict the weather.

"Smashing." Was his sarcasm apparent? "At least there's only three of them to face," he swiftly told Luce, "not all five, seven counting our parents—the ancients."

"Seven? D-do they do this a lot?" she quietly choked out, understandably anxious (given the interruption on the heels of the intimacies just shared between them) and huddled within his bed coverings, those enchanting, sky-blue eyes that reminded him of home—the splendor found above the stunning aspects he never tired of gazing at present only in Yorkshire where he grew up, and where most of his family still remained—downright   captivating.   "Arrive without warning?"

Now wasn't the time to tell her how he tended the store during fall and winter, and every other spring and summer, trading off with Clay who traveled to the city during the hotter months to see if he could locate any new specimens recently arrived via boat or bird.

"At least once a year." He released one cheek to kiss the flushed skin while dragging his hand down, past her collarbone, over the gentle swell of her breast, to anchor at her waist, giving what little comfort he could.

"Drowsed late!" he called out, weighing the fear lingering in her expression. "Be down post-haste!"

Was she afraid of being caught in his bed?

He had half a mind to let it happen, call forth his boisterous siblings, bid them to dash up the stairs, to catch him and Luce *in flagrante*.

She would have no choice but to marry him, then.

But he didn't want her that way—without a choice.

"If I meet them quickly, they won't come up." He squeezed her waist and climbed from the bed to pluck a shirt off a peg, his bottom half still covered by yesterday's pants. Drawing the shirt over his head, he glanced down at his bare feet. No help for it; the rest would take too long. Couldn't risk Thorne hazarding the steps to drag his slow arse downstairs.

As he dressed, she pushed up to sitting, watching him with eyes gone luminous, and still very uncertain.

"Mew."

Calf rubs meant to comfort? He picked up the cat and plopped him in her lap. "She needs you more.

"Were it my decision?" he told her quietly but as intently as he dared. "I would love to introduce you to them. But 'tis your choice. I want you to stay, with me and Barnabas. Making laughter and memories together. But I do not want you embarrassed or shamed into it by the unexpected busyheads downstairs. Remain up here if you are not yet ready to have your future decided with such haste."

"Brier Edgar! Coming up there and tossing you out the window in ten...nine..."

"Only a moment more!" He leaned over the bed and brushed her hair back. Covering the greenish-yellow cheek with one hand, he bent to sup from her lips. Two seconds only. A lifetime would be too short.

"Seven...six..."

He started to rush down the stairs, but at the doorway, he paused, turned back.

She still looked befuddled, as though too much had been heaped upon her at once. "I know. We Chapmans are a lot to take in at once." He nodded his head in a semblance of a bow, a show of respect. Something he would have done had he been courting her in truth, a lifetime ago, before he chose his great-great-grandfather's way of life instead of the more idle one he'd been raised with.

"Four..."

"'Tis your decision." He'd already laid himself bare. "Just know that, for myself, I would escort you down there on my arm, if I could."

"Two..."

"Mind your impatience!" he growled toward the stairway.

He blew her a kiss that he hoped danced through the motes in the air and landed smack on her still swollen cheek before he braced himself to greet his siblings and the inquisition he knew was coming.

11

CHRISTMAS SNACKS >^..^<

———◦○◦———

"IMPATIENT KNOBS!" Brier's retreating voice carried easily to her in the relative quiet of his lodgings. "Ye may see my arsehole between—"

"The middle of your buttocks!" One of his brothers finished the crude greeting, all three— nay, *four*—of them laughing at what must be familial humor.

Family. Something that had been missing from Lucinda's life for a very long while.

"Why do you not look delighted to see us?" Eve asked, confusion evident in her tone. "We bring our Christmas presence, if not Christmas presents."

"And a wonderful gift that is," Brier answered. "Sleeping hard, I was."

"No wonder." One of the brothers. "You

adorned even the back rooms this year. *You*, who has hated Christmas for an age?"

"Not...hated." Brier's voice grew fainter. "Simply not celebrated. Not...this..."

Legs crossed beneath the bed covers, kitty nestled in the crook, she strained to hear more over the frantic thumping of her heart.

To no avail.

"Merr?"

Never have I enjoyed a Christmas more, he'd told her yesterday, during their simple meal made extravagant by the company and conversation.

Every word I have spoken to you is truth.

"Rrroow!"

Still in a dazing, 'twas a moment—or mayhap minutes—before Luce noticed the slight prick of claws resting upon her forearm, the piercing pressure deepening until she shook herself out of the idle-headedness and scratched nails over furry jaws and beneath one very stubborn feline chin. "Give me back my arm, you rapscallion."

Still, she stared in the direction of the stairway, where Brier had disappeared around a tight corner before descending.

"Mercy me. Stay here and make memories?" As what?

If it were as his assistant, he wouldn't have invited you upstairs.

If it were as his mistress, he wouldn't have invited you downstairs.

Hugging those thoughts to herself, Luce debated.

Her future balanced precariously on the slimmest precipice she'd known. Did she keep to his room, concealing herself, thereby taking the predictable, yet uninspired path? That of companion, of underappreciated servant?

"Meeow. Mewrr?"

Her fingers braved traveling from the cat and beyond the warm coverings that still held the scent of the man who'd held her all night. She stroked the mattress where he'd lain. *Brier*. Who'd caressed her so splendidly this morning.

Or did she, conversely, take the greatest leap of her life? Launch off that intimidating precipice and fly? Trusting the man she had known such a short, yet exultant, time to catch her?

I want to jump. To soar straight into his arms.

"Reeoww!"

Seemed their feline agreed with her choice, but when Luce threw off the covers, ready to head downstairs, 'twas to the realization she had naught but her night-rail in the vicinity. Which made any downward journey a thousand times more challenging.

So she bundled up in a jacket of Brier's, found hanging over the privacy screen, and made it halfway down the stairs before her pluck expired. So she flopped down where she stood, hindquarters meeting the wooden step, and crossed her arms tight across her middle.

"There now." If anyone thought to look, they would see her. While not visible to those in the store, anyone who ventured into the back rooms had a clear view of their brother's now *decidedly* loose Luce.

She choked on her own spit at the thought and then sat up a little straighter.

Barnabas butted against her back, urging her to her feet and the rest of the way. "Meerrrrreeeee*owww*!!"

"No, sir," she told the cat in a whisper—who one would swear, just *huffed* as he slid on by, tail stiffly erect.

At the bottom of the stairs, he gave her a narrow-eyed glare before stalking off, toward the indistinct voices—no longer easily audible now that the siblings need not yell to be heard.

———◦◦◦———

Ho-hum.

Humans. Why did they not listen?

Was not his important self trying to nudge the female toward the discovery of her belongings?

Had he not planted himself in the cold, dark, stench-filled alley yesterday, claws piercing the bag his new fierce friend had left, claiming it? Protecting it? Waiting and waiting and waiting...

For preposterous humans who took an absurd amount of time to even begin searching for the worthy feline who deigned to protect their abode from mice, rats and various varmints and vermin?

Humedy-hum-hum.

Unwilling to condescend further, for his patience had quite reached its end, Barnabas brushed past their new female—who absolutely refused to listen, to heed his entreaties. Stubborn lass.

He decided instead to lure his landlord's younger brother outside; he'd already identified their visitors by scent, possessor of such an accomplished sniffer and all.

Barnabas utterly *thrived* when the one called Clayton came to stay in the shop and play merchant for a time, all those creepers and crawlers the man liked to collect?

The "specimens" Barnabas preferred to think of as *snacks...*

"HAMPSHIRE HOGS AND SUFFOLK SHEEP, *who are you*?"

The black-haired stunner, her skin unfashionably dark, sped forward upon spying Lucinda. Strong-tea-colored eyes opened wide, her astonished smile quickly following.

Brier's sister—Eve?—jerked to a halt partway up the steps and gasped, her smile faltering to a stern frown "Oh my goodness." She waved fingers at the side of her own face, mirroring Luce's bruise. "Please tell me my brother didn't—"

"Nay! How could you even *think*—" Fierce protectiveness swamped her, squashed out the earlier hesitation. "How could you *ask* such? Brier would never—"

"I know. I *know*. But..." The female, dressed as one making morning calls on those of elevated status, dropped to her knees on the nearest step and grasped Luce's hands with her gloved ones, just then noticing the wraps. "I know. Forgive my runaway mouth. 'Tis simply a shock. To see a *female*. Here. With him. What *did* happen? For now that I look closer upon your countenance, even I can discern no fist did that. And these bandages?" Lightly, she lifted Luce's hands. "Are *you* all right?"

'Twas on the tip of Luce's tongue to ask just how Brier's sister would know of fist-size bruises. But the effusive Eve wasn't close to finished.

"How did you meet? Where?" The unlined face and open expression showed her to be substantially younger than her brothers. Younger than Luce. "When did you marry?"

"*Marry?*" Luce gulped. "We aren't— Have yet to—" At the open curiosity, the lack of censure on the other woman's face, Luce's tongue kept flapping. "We did occupy... Ahm, we didn't bed together. I mean to say, we did. But he didn't *bed* me. We didn't— Did not—"

"Halt. Do not distress yourself. 'Tis not my place to censure another's actions."

"You don't understand. I was in a carriage accident." Luce thought it best to forbore relaying the whole chased-by-a-beast thing. "I was injured. Everything was closed. With the storm and the ice—"

"But you suffer no other severe injuries?" Luce shook her head, unable to do anything else, sheer wonder rolling over her at the warm reception Eve gave, welcoming her presence in her brother's life. "Please, say no more." Eve smoothed her thumbs over the wrappings. "How I have wished for the time when I would see Brier with another female. I care not how you met. Just knowing he encouraged you to remain. That"—her gaze slid upward, toward the bed they had so recently occupied. "Well."

The other woman fairly beamed, released Luce's hands and rose up on her knees to give Luce an unexpected hug. When she leaned back, the smile was still in place. "I'm Eve, the youngest. What is your name? Pigs and puddles, I cannot believe I didn't ask you that before. You shall meet the rest of us soon enough, I am sure. And though you haven't had time *yet*, shall I wish you happy? The two of you *are...*" Her eyebrows angled toward the *bed*. "Right?"

And there it was.

He had all but invited her to trape down the stairs and introduce herself to his family, but had he mentioned marriage? Explicitly? She couldn't recall.

But he had spoken of a lifetime together, of making memories and laughter.

"We only just met." *And yet you spent the night in his arms? In his bed?*

"Adzooks, what has that to do with anything?" Eve rhapsodized. "*Our* parents met at Papa's betrothal ball to another and they both stole off until *their* parents agreed to the match, or mismatch, as it were. A potential marquis—"

"M-marquis?"

"He was fourth in line at the time, had discounted the possibility himself, but came into the title and lands after several unexpected occurrences. That and far sooner than anyone could have anticipated." Eve waved it off as though the news were naught but lint to be flicked. "And Mama the third daughter of the local magistrate, the family only invited to help make even numbers—and because I gather her eldest sister was friends to Papa's *original* intended. As to their union? Married forty-two years and still unfashionably *in love*."

"And this, after only *one* meeting?" Luce could scarce believe it. "Pray, share more."

Why? Do you need to hear of another's folly, a successful one? Before committing to one yourself?

"I gather theirs was a rare *two*-season scandal," Eve confided, "thanks to the fray his original betrothed kept on everyone's lips. Though I think Thorne and Sharpe may have usurped—"

A jumble of strong footsteps sounded beyond their cozy spot.

Three gentlemen jostled around the corner, all stopping at once.

Brier, barefoot in between the two others. Easy to identify even had her gaze not sought him out, over and above the other two who resembled him mightily, even though one of them had lighter hair than the rest of the siblings.

None of the three newly arrived siblings appeared travel worn. His two brothers attired more elegantly than one might expect for an early-morning call after such a blanket of muck and mud covered London and the surrounding roadways, given the lingering ice and storms. Their Hessians, dark pantaloons and embroidered waistcoats, beneath fine-fitting waistcoats indeed, contrasted sharply with Brier's modest pants and shirt—and naught else.

There was no mistaking the brotherly similarities between the three. The way they stood, held themselves. Their very posture—aye, their impressive presence—that reached out and fairly delivered an unexpected blow to her middle.

Especially when Brier said with obvious pleasure, "You came down."

His relief warmed her heart and calmed the riotous churning clanging in her chest the interruption—not to mention the sight of him —caused.

"What, ho? And *who* is this?" The slightly younger one, with hair that couldn't decide whether to be brown or blond, kept glancing between Brier and herself and just grinned.

"I did not get very far," she admitted, keeping her gaze steady on his.

"So you finally took a mistress? You bawdry old dog!" The other one, with hair dark as sin and sun-hewn features knuckled Brier's head, hard enough to make him wince. "Certainly took you long enough."

"Mistress, my arse. He's not the type. And don't insult the lady." The other one reached around Brier to punch the darker one in the arm. Then he addressed Brier. "What have you been keeping from us? Have you gone and got yourself buckled without telling—"

"That is beyond enough." Beside her, Eve swept to her feet and marched forward, whispering something to Brier as she hooked an arm through each of the others' and tugged them back the way they'd just come, away from the back rooms and toward the shop. "Out with you both," she ordered in a booming voice, despite her smaller stature. "Bri does not need either of *you* distractions distracting him from his mission."

Amidst their good-natured grumbling, diminishing by the moment as they retreated, Brier approached, his haphazard clothing and mousled hair—plus his lack of footgear—gave evidence for his brother's assumption. "Were you going to keep walking?" he asked quietly as he reached her, and she tilted her head upward to meet his downturned gaze. "Were you intending to come find me, or did Eve catch and halt you unawares?"

"Given how I had perched upon this tread with no serious thoughts of leaving, could we say *both*?"

"You were not aiming to escape, without goodbye, were you?"

"Nothing of the sort." Lucinda leaned forward and took possession of his hand. She tugged and drew him down beside her. "Thanks to my new boots..." She kicked out one foot, the thought crossing her mind that mayhap she had stolen them from Eve and would need to make apologies later. "My brave feet brought me this far, but the cowardish rest of me forestalled further progress. What did she just say to you? If it isn't overly forward of me—"

"Of course you may ask." He gave her hand a comforting squeeze, his lips tilting in a rueful grin as he settled next to her on the narrow tread. "Said she would never forgive me if I did not convince you to stay. That if I did anything to bungle things with you, she and Rose would join forces and CHAPMAN'S would be out a fragrance supplier *and* bottle painter."

He took her hand and placed it upon the top of his bent leg, just above his knee. He began tracing over the back of it, his gaze never leaving hers. "You will stay? Consider making this your home?"

"I am conflicted, I admit. I want to," she said, almost unwillingly, "but after so short an acquaintance does it not seem the most egregious, asinine, foolhardy—"

He pressed his hand down over hers. "'Tis enough, I assure you. I would prefer to think of it as daring, perhaps, definitely venturesome."

How did he calm her fears? Settle the uncertainty brimming in her gaze, along with the (did he but hope) yearning?

She flipped her hand until their palms met, curved her fingers between his. "I cannot imagine what would have become of me, had you not opened your doors and rescued me."

"If I recall, you banged them open and bolted yourself inside, for which I will be forever grateful." He shifted to better face her, bringing one leg inelegantly up and around so that she—to a degree—nestled within his thighs. "And, Lucinda? It is you who rescued me, who opened my heart, that which had been closed off for years."

One silent tear tracked down her cheek, despite her soft smile. He lifted their joined hands to brush it away.

Then decided just to jabber everything out

before he could stop himself. "'Tis too soon—us; you and me. I know it is. Utterly insane. But I cannot imagine you leaving. Cannot fathom *not* seeing you again, not talking with you. Laughing together. I feel so very at ease when I'm with you and yet—

"Yet, my body has been on a razor's edge since the moment you burst into CHAPMAN'S. I desire you fiercely. Would like for you to remain. *Need* for you to remain." He pulled in a quick breath, leaned down for a long kiss, and then finished—before she could further protest the absurdity of making a decision of such import upon so brief an acquaintance. "Take whatever time you need, ascertain for yourself what manner of man I am day in and day out. You will see I am steady and true."

"You have already shown to be both."

"Lucinda, do you imagine you could be happy here? With me?"

"Reow!" His cat bounded over from the direction his siblings had disappeared, hopping up on the nearest step, to rub against their legs.

Above the furious hammering of his heart, he heard Clay give an astonished whistle. "Bri will never believe what his cat just dragged in."

"Here now, let me have a look," Thorne demanded. "Rather tattered is it not?"

Eve hushed them both even as she exclaimed, "Is that a valise? Someone's night bag?"

Barnabas purred louder than bolting horses.

Brier ignored them all. Released Luce's hand to reach under the feline's belly and haul the cat into his lap, awkward though it was. Furious chin scratches kept him in place. "And this worthless piece of fangs and fur. We're a pair, you know. If I cannot tempt you to abandon thoughts of companioning old cantankerous biddies, can he?"

"Merrrow!"

She slowly rubbed her fingers over the purring kitty's neck, keeping her attention focused downward, on their hands, where they both petted Barnabas, the tips of their fingers crossing paths every few seconds.

One full breath. Then another. A third. His chest lifting, stomach sinking as he waited. Toes stretched and pinched together. He fought his impatience. Sought to give her time.

Seven breaths later—that could have been an hour—she met his eyes again, her attention flitting to his mouth. "Stay? As your assistant?"

He growled.

"As your *mistress*, you mean?" The soft utterance, whispered as though they shared a secret, had him giving a hearty laugh.

"No, you precious puzzle-head, as my wife."

"Oh. Because in truth, I was considering the other."

He dumped the protesting cat off his lap, brought his legs back together and angled his torso over the stairs until she leaned back upon the treads and he had her caged within his arms. "I accept."

At the slow caress of his lips over her cheek, she giggled. "Now you're the bufflehead. Just what do you think you accept?"

"I accept your acceptance to be my mistress. But only until you are ready to be my wife."

12

GIFTS AND GLOATS

———◦◦———

"Delighted," said Clayton. Who, eschewing Luce's fumbling attempts to address him properly, told her *not* to call him Lord Clayton—"Or, heaven forfend, 'Mr. Chapman', 'ere a handful of other male relatives jump to answer."

She stood in the middle of the shop, facing Brier's younger brother wearing her borrowed dress and gifted boots. Hair tamed into a neat coil, stomach pleasantly full and nerves only slightly aflutter. The other vocal, teasing Chapmans hovered closer to the entrance, most everything they had just unloaded already repacked ahead of their imminent departure.

Not quite two hours ago, after noodling with Brier, sprawled upon the stairs, long enough that her back protested and Thorne's risqué observations grew ribald enough—and were spoken sufficiently loud she and Brier were meant to hear—Brier leveraged off her with a groan.

After a few more heated kisses, lingering hugs and nuzzles once they were both back on their feet, along with whispered awe and amazement (and a few heartfelt promises from Brier, ones that warmed her down to her soul), they had been encouraged to go upstairs and take a moment for themselves (which Luce translated into "get thyself attired properly").

Upon their return downstairs, they all made haste partaking of the bounty the siblings had laid out.

Their "plates" were a hash of actual plates and a couple of pans, Brier not having five of everything since for years he had eaten alone. He smilingly withstood the chiding of his siblings when he refused to use merchandise for sale, which would have meant matching plates for all. Lucinda glowed at that, given how willing he had been to grant her anything in the store she desired when inviting her to create a holiday atmosphere in the back of his shop.

The fantastical meal was vibrant and varied, a true gift for one accustomed to eating repetitive, unadorned offerings. In addition to the more traditional fare Eve and Clayton claimed respon-sibility for, Thorne's recent travels contributed some rather unique items: lobster and squid, pineapple (so very extravagant!) plus other bright fruits and even a particular nut she had never seen, much less eaten, before.

To Luce's ever-growing astonishment, the siblings accepted her presence with nary a blink, inviting her into their conversations, entertaining her with their familial banter, all while avoiding asking anything overly personal of her. 'Twas as though upon realizing how utterly *recent* her and their brother's acquaintance truly was, they took care not to pry or embarrass either of them further. Astonishing, that, given how their first few seconds together had gone.

Once the contents of plates—and pans—were demolished, and the "plates" themselves polished clean, the visiting trio immediately began gathering their things, stating they would remove to their purchased lodgings, needing to do what they could to "foster a most positive outcome" between her and Brier. This last stated decisively by Eve, giving her the impression that the timing of their departure had been determined previously—likely while she and Brier busied themselves "with a loud bit of slip-slop as they go at it" (another of Thorne's clacks that Eve quickly hushed).

So, sooner than Luce would ever have expected, given the distance traveled and still relatively early hour, the siblings readied to leave after bellies were full. But they did not depart until each took a solitary moment to welcome Luce to the family, starting with Clayton.

"Utterly relieved more than I can say to see Brier smiling again," he continued now, standing so very confidently before Luce while the others waited patiently by the door. "It's been far longer than any one of us wanted to acknowledge since his countenance showed anything save stoic acceptance or outright ennui.

"May I?" Clayton held his arms out, and—while betwattlement battled with discomfiture—Luce nodded. And found herself wrapped in a solid, brotherly hug that brought a hitch to her breath and several frenzied blinks to clear her eyes. "No one shall hear from my lips quite how today transpired." He spoke the promise quietly, for her ears alone. "*You* appear to be what—*who* —he has needed for years." He gave her a small squeeze and then brought his arms down, step-ping back to give her a friendly grin. "Please, come visit us and the ancients at Everling when you deem yourself ready."

Giving her a jaunty nod, he backed away to join the others.

So touched she thought she'd burst, all Luce could do was stand there, hand over her pounding heart.

Then it was Eve's turn, the energetic female bounding over as soon as Clayton left.

"Did I hear Clay mention Yorkshire to you?"

"Yorkshire?"

"Everling Hall. That's where we hail from." A slight flush covered her cheekbones when she dimpled. "Well, more like *hide from* society during the worst of times—or best per Sharpe, who has a tendency to be overly proud of everyone's scandalizing accomplishments—"

"Scandalizing?" Not quite the word usually applied toward achievements.

"Oh, you know," Eve answered airily, brushing off any hint of concern. "All the sullen hum and buzz that seems to follow us about—and without any real effort on our parts at all. Aye, do come visit"—she fluttered her fingers near Luce's cheek—"as soon and the swelling is gone, the rainbow has faded, yes? No sense inciting curiosity where none need be encouraged."

Eve beamed at her, her already animated face coming alight with her smile. "Oh, pigs in puddles and bunnies in burrows, another sister! Scarce can I believe it."

Sister? Said with such utter certainty. And without vows or anything approaching thus said yet between her and Brier. What if he changed his mind? What if she did?

Bunnies would fly and pigs would burrow before such a thing occurred, and you know it.

Still, caution needed reminded. "Please remember, we have yet to stand before clergy and speak..." Luce could not help but glance over Eve's shoulder to where the three brothers huddled, the low hum of male voices such a new and welcome experience.

Previously dormant parts of Luce flamed to seething life the moment Brier caught her gaze. Eyes glinting, he said loudly, "We *will*, be assured of that, Luce." Proving that he had kept one ear on what his siblings said to her. "After giving me your agreement earlier and muzzling me till we both broke out in a sweat, do not seek a way out."

A wave of heat rolled over her, her lips tingling anew.

"Earlier agreement?" Eve squealed, practically jumping in her delight. "So you *are* to be wed? Of a certainty! How soon? Where? Will you—"

"Not so fast, Midsummer," Clayton interrupted. "You—"

"How I hate that name." Eve aimed daggers at him.

"Nay, do not harry her," Brier said, retrieving one of the travel bags waiting by the door and shoving it into his brother's middle. "Neither Eve nor my new lady, for Luce has yet to agree to *everything*."

Their sibling affection and sparring, so reminiscent of her early years with her sister, prompted Luce to reply. "*For the nonce*"—she could not help but say this quite flippantly—"I have agreed to be his *mistress*."

Eve sputtered.

Clay chuckled.

Thorne guffawed, slapping Clay on the back.

"What did I tell you? That's twenty quid to my palm from yours, and I want it by nightfall."

Brier just stood by, full lips mostly straight, while his dark eyes glimmered. She fairly *felt* his mirth, his approval, ebb her direction as though they alone shared a unique and silent bond of their own.

Moments before the rackety trio left, Thorne cleared his throat. "My turn, I believe. For I have yet to welcome Brier's new mistress to the family."

His boots clicked smartly across the shop as he neared. And—accepting of her the past hour or more or not—Luce couldn't halt the fidgets that slammed her middle as the tall, rather daunting, reputed "pirate" approached.

"Miss Thomalin." He possessed himself of her hand and actually *bowed* over it. Brushed the fingers of his opposite hand gently over the bandage before giving just the tips of her fingers a slight squeeze—and the rest of her a devilish wink from beneath the inky hair fallen forward over his brow.

"Despaired of him ever coming close to a female again," he declared in a quiet rumble as he straightened. "Glad to know his cock's still in working fashion. Had—"

"Thorne!"

"Thorneton!"

"Buzzard-brain."

Evidently not quiet enough, given the strident complaints directed his way.

The ones Thorne ignored easier than she. "Had a wager with Sharpe that Brier's bauble— er, commodity"—he modified, showing he had at least heard his siblings' protests, if not totally taking them to heart—"had shriveled off by now." He rubbed his chin, wrinkled his nose in a sign of irritation. "Relieved that isn't the state of things. But damn. Suppose I owe *him* now. At least I earned as much from the youngling earlier."

By now, the slight hint of red that worked its way over the tips of Brier's ears snared her attention. Knowing that his *commodities* and other parts of an intimate nature were definitely not shriveled, she tried to give him one of those confidence-instilling smiles he'd been so generously giving her since they awoke to the bustle of visitors.

But then Clay shifted, bent to retrieve more belongings to add to his load before departing—

"My bag!"

Joy seized Luce at the site of the tattered, worn travel valise that had been with her for years, ever since her thirteenth birthday when her parents gave her one to match her older sister's.

Forget Thorne and his intimidating, piratical bearing, she flew across the shop and took hold of the bag Clayton held out at her cry. "And it's not been beggared!"

No one had thieved her items, for after hours of travel, years of so few possessions, she knew its heft and bulk and the arrangement of every single treasure inside.

As she hugged it tight, lips trembling, being so full of wonder she could no longer speak, Brier placed an arm about her shoulders and his opposite hand beneath the bag. "This is *yours*? You are certain?"

A sharp nod was all she could manage.

"Explain this. Where did the lot of you come by her things?"

"No need to bark at us, Bri. Did—"

"Merrow!"

THOROUGHLY SATED after jumping up to the counter earlier and helping himself to the remaining nibbles not yet packed away—heh, heh—Barnabas clawed his way up Thorne's buckskins...

To some inventive, most indecent language (that fair made his adorable pointy little ears fold inward to shield his delicate sensibilities), Barnabas climbed and clambered until he rode atop the man's shoulders. Once in place, furry back legs dangling (claws engaged and aiding his already impeccable balance), he glared at his motley band of absurd humans.

The lot of them, really! "ME-OW!"

He sighed, listening, for now that his belly

was full, he cared naught about bestirring himself to chase after pesky rodents. Nay, that sort of effort—required of his already well-proven, worthy self—was best left for another week. Another month, mayhap.

"Did you not hear Clay earlier?" Thorne's shoulders vibrated when he spoke, almost as good as a satisfying belly rub. "This one"—Barns's deserving self purred at the chin scratch his master's oldest brother imparted—"hauled it inside shortly after we breached your door this morn."

If feline snouts could gloat, he would have. *Aye, I did. Dragged it all the dog-blame way from the alley to the front door as soon as I smelled younger brother's ever-present, purr-inducing satchel of snacks.*

"He did." Clay—preferably known as the Snack Man—sounded impressed (as well he should). "Circled my ankles till I offered to let him outside, then yammered at me until I opened the front door, not the back. A few moments later, he came lumbering up with it."

Lumbering? His tail flicked, snapped Thorne in the ear.

"Ow!"

I do not lumber.

More like swagger and strut.

"Barnabas!" His landlord's woman was awash with delight. "You are utterly smashing! The veritable best!"

Of course he was.

His new female launched herself (no lumbering there either) toward him. And 'twas chinnies galore till he nearly rolled off his perch in a state of duly adored bliss.

———◦○◦———

FOR BRIER, the rest of the day passed in a haze of combined joy and disbelief, as both he and Luce found reasons, or created ones, to touch. To brush against each other. Reaching for the taper, scrambling for a jar of ink, stretching for a penknife. Arguing with Barnabas over table crumbs.

Seemingly innocent brushes of one body against another that he suspected they each felt in decisively non-innocent ways.

After so many years of silence (cantankerous cats counted naught) and stillness, refusing to succumb to old sorrows or current self-insulation, the near-constant sharing with another—words, thoughts, *touches*...

It made him thankful.

Thankful he was alive. Thankful he had chosen the quiet, steadfast "rebellion" of seeing CHAPMAN'S successful year after year, while his more vocal, more memorable, siblings instead chose to shine, to scandalize and racket about society while he remained in the shadows.

How could he have known such contentment

—such *rousing* contentment, he thought, pulling Luce into his embrace late that evening when the rest of the city was no doubt already abed— would burst through his unlocked door on such a dismal, drizzly eve? Light his life up like a Vaux-hall firework mere days before the globe cele-brated the birth of Christ?

His clock had chimed midnight not long before. How had the hours passed so swiftly?

Her arms went around his waist and she tucked her head beneath his chin and held him tight. They stood by the stairs, in the near dark after just extinguishing both candles, slowly wavering in place. "Part of me fears going to sleep tonight," she murmured against his chest, the heat of her breath causing more than his fists at her back to clench.

"Afraid your beast might return?" His words were barely audible.

"Nay, no longer," she whispered on a yawn, moving her arms until they wound over his shoulders and around his neck, bringing her face closer to his. "Afraid I will wake and find this all a dream."

"This?"

She gripped him harder, pressed her mouth upon his lips, her tongue seeking entrance to slide against his until they were both gasping for breath and grasping each other.

By the time she pulled back to whisper, "You and I. Our future—with each other, together," his palms were firm against her hinterlands, bringing the special wonder of Lovely Lucinda as close to his body as one could while still clothed. "Does it not feel as a dream to you?"

He released the greedy clasp of his fingers to stroke them down her thighs and back up to her waist. Then he brushed both against the top of her head, lodged one behind her neck, curving his fingers over her nape while the other spread wide against her back. "No dream, this. I am far too awake and you are far too luscious and real, and I will continue to hold you tight every night for the rest of our lives so that each time you awake, you will worry not."

She finally released the clutch around his shoulders, brought her fingers to cup either side of his face, her thumbs roving over his skin in the dark. "That is one promise I shall be happy to endure."

"Endure?" He mock growled and was rewarded with the delight of her carefree giggle. So vastly different from the frightened miss of just a few days prior.

"Endure with happiness imbuing every ounce of my being," she whispered against one ear, sounding infinitely more alert than she had only moments ago.

"Mew?"

He felt the slight bump against his ankle, telling him Barnabas had finally come back in and they could lock the door and return upstairs. "Aye, Barns, it is time."

She leaned down to scoop the cat into her arms. "To bed?"

"Assuredly," he said with so much satisfaction, it was a wonder his chest could contain the fullness filling his heart. "We must away, *dear* maiden..." He took two steps backward, guiding their feet to the stairs. "To sleep, dear one."

Tiring of being docile and unargumentative —for once—their feline leapt down and raced upward. "To slumber and snuggle?"

'Twas an easy matter to guide his arm around her waist, keeping her close and protected, as they ascended to his lodgings.

Dodging a sprawled-out bit of laze-about fluff at the top, Brier lifted her in his arms and made it safely to their bed, where he placed her upon it before following her down. "Aye, Lovely Luce, to *our* dream. One never ending."

All's well that ends well. Goodnight.

EPILOGUE I: THE BEAST

———◦———

THE MAN-BEAST WATCHED from afar three months later, as Mr. and the new Mrs. Brier Chapman (as they chose to be known in London, forsaking the more appropriate *Lord and Lady Brier Chapman*) descended from the Marquis of Everling's traveling carriage.

Today marked the end of their extended wedding trip to Yorkshire, where the rest of the sundry Chapmans tended to reside, when not being industrious in London, piratical over the seas, or engaging in one of the other outlandish modes of activity the extravagant family members were known for.

Today also marked the beginning of their new life together.

His heart ached at the sight of them holding hands, happy and free of care, especially after the terror he'd unwittingly caused, simply following her home that wretched, awful night, to ensure her safety from the vile ones who might steal the very breath from her lungs.

While waiting for their trunks to be unloaded, the couple nuzzled noses and laughed at something one of them said, making the pang in his chest deepen. He was ready to return to his own mate, without letting this lingering commitment draw him away ever again. Now that he'd seen his duty—the responsibility he'd felt for the female unfortunate enough to be caught up in things she had no notion of—discharged to his (and doubtless her own) satisfaction, he could halt his rounds this direction, no longer detour to and from his club, checking on her safety and happiness.

Brier Chapman, the Marquis of Everling's third born, and his wickedly observant feline had seen to both.

"Sentimental fool," the not-oft beastly man remarked with a mocking grin, chiding himself and acknowledging the truth of the words.

For ever since finding and marrying his own dear Francy months earlier, Erasmus Hammond, a marquis in his own right, had altered his thinking and perceptions on just about everything. His entire outlook on life.

One truth his beloved Francy had convinced him of held sway: Not all beasts are bad.

EPILOGUE II: BRIER AND LUCINDA

C-R-A-S-H!

Lucinda yelped the same instant Brier bristled, "Not again! Blame cat."

Frustrated gazes connected.

"Poor Will," she whispered, tugging at a strand of hair near her mouth; the humidity had made several stick to her cheek today. She pulled it free and twined it back around the knot containing the rest.

Both of them were knee deep in straw padding, flung from the crate of merchandise they emptied in the back of the shop.

'Twas nearing the hour when they locked the doors. The incessant autumn rains the last two days had kept most customers mired at home, not venturing outside to visit CHAPMAN & SONS, no matter that several shipments arranged by Thorne had arrived yesterday and today. They had been working on unpacking the last of it.

"Shall I go put him to rights this time?" Brier lightly touched the shiny finish—solid black this year—on one equine from the latest team of horse figurines they had just uncovered, then gingerly stepped from the mess. "While you finish up here?"

"Certainly. Sounds as though his poor head may be lolling about."

"*Helmet*, sweetheart," he corrected, gaining his feet and making haste toward the store.

She raised her voice, intending it carry into the shop—where one of the Chapman family "triplets" (the other two being Shakes and Spear) still clanged and groaned, thanks to their mischievous tabby. "Stop climbing Will, Barns!"

With care, she unearthed the rest of the goods, half her attention on the arguing pair out front.

"Barnabas, you fiendish feline, you practically broke his face with this latest topple!"

"Merrowwl!"

"Did Will land on his nose again?" she asked over her shoulder, cringing at the thought.

"*Visor* or *bevor*, Luce, not 'nose'." She chuckled, thinking how it had become a jest between them—her mangling the proper terms. "And aye, skewed and bent now." Brier went back to addressing their cat, his words sounding rather strangled. "Doubtful I can pound them straight again, not now that *you* have dispatched him for a *fourth* time—"

"Gwrrrwl?"

"Nay," answered her husband of nine months. "Doing your duty as CHAPMAN'S official Ratter the last three weeks does *not* give you the right to clamber up Will, or jump from the counter—or the curtains"—she bit back a smile when his voice started growling a bit like their irascible cat's—"and destroy what Luce and I put together—"

"BrrRRREOW!"

"No, even if that last one looked to weigh upward of a bloody—*very bloody*—pound."

"Merr."

Luce smiled for she could practically see man and cat in a duel of wits and wills.

"Speaking of weight..." she told the crate, "you...are going to...make me work for this one..." With only a tiny grunt, she eased free the last, largest bundled package from the depths. "Just what are you?"

Already the well-padded delivery of goods had yielded four full sets of Brier's prized horses (with the adorably tiny wreaths about their necks), a lovely collection of small frames—one of which Brier insisted was hers; saying it belonged upstairs, surrounding the precious miniature of her sister and propped on the mantel, where he'd created a place in between his ring and the striped rock he'd found as a child, on a long walk with a long-deceased favored uncle.

She pulled the wrapping from the heavy bundle and revealed three very stately carvings: lions made from stone or marble, each in a different pose. The one she held now stood on its hind feet with one front paw raised, mouth open as though to proclaim its grandeur. The intricacies were easily beyond anything she'd seen thus far. Why, one could fairly touch the soft mane, so exquisite was the detail. Hear the roar from the open mouth...

The table statues had been requested by a customer looking for just the right gifts for several family members, as she'd told them. According to the note tucked inside the crate, Thorne had found these in Italy.

After ascertaining all three were in impeccable condition, Luce wrapped them again and wiped her hands on a nearby towel, already thinking ahead. "I shall send round a note, let Lady Blakely know they have arrived."

———◦◦◦———

The Following Week

FINISHING NUNCHEON—SNEAKING Barns more than was wise—Brier hustled down the stairs to continue his efforts putting away things he and Luce had let accumulate in the storeroom. What a boon—to have a *partner*, a friend and lover for all seasons. He licked his lips, recalling where they had been a few hours ago.

His lady—his Lovely Luce—bringing not only joy and contentment back to his days, but passion to his nights as well.

Humming to himself, he started with the topmost crate—where they'd taken to keeping customer orders—to relocate those to the newest wall of shelves he'd finished yesterday.

The other wall they'd laden with supplies for the less fortunate, as he and Luce took to heart her plight upon reaching London and now helped others when they could.

His tuneless hum stumbled on a chuckle when he heard her talking to the medieval metal out front. His heart light, he resumed his efforts, arranging several more orders on a shelf before he stood back to consider. *Hmmm.* "By weight and size or alphabetically?"

A sharp rap on the back door pulled him that direction. *I will see what Luce thinks.*

Recognizing the sound, he unlatched and opened the door. "Lord Blakely." Brier greeted the severely dressed marquis standing in the somewhat sordid alley.

Lord Blakely, who knew more than most peers about the workings of the seedier parts of their city.

"Chapman, have you met my brother, Lord Hammond? Nash, this is Lord Brier Chapman, Everling's... What? Third born?"

Brier slipped outside so they wouldn't disturb any shoppers best left to their own thoughts—and not the dangerous ones sometimes swirling beneath the surface of the words he and Blakely had taken to exchanging over the last few months.

"Aye, third." Brier took in the shaggy-haired brother of the refined Blakely, strands brushing his shoulders and falling forward over one eye until he scraped them back behind one ear and nodded, glancing behind Brier to the door. "In trade, eh? And managing to live your own life without scandal-mongers hounding you?"

"I do indeed." Brier had a pleasant, if cordial, relationship with Blakely, who maintained distance from everyone in public. His younger brother, now? At the loose posture and looser neckcloth, Brier felt his body relax. "Cannot say the same for the rest of us Chapmans, as I'm sure you know, but my wife and I have a good life. Meaningful to each other and hopefully to the mercantile's patrons." His gaze roved to take in both men, Lord Blakely's wife being one of their frequent customers. "And unlike most Londoners in trade, I can always whisk my lady off to Yorkshire if we need a holiday or Papa summons us for a game of kittle-pins or pitch and hustle."

Blakely gave a rare laugh—one that reached

his eyes. "I sometimes forget what an undaunted, festivous character your father can be. He was friends with mine—*ours*—before..." Blakely and his brother turned solemn as he finished. "I met Lord Everling as a child. Take pleasure in his company every chance you may."

"I shall." Brier knew there was more to this visit than casual blather. "How goes the other matter we discuss? Any progress?"

Blakely and those in his employ worked to keep the dangerous city streets a little less so.

"Not as much as we demmed well need." Lord Hammond spit behind him after uttering this as though his thoughts had turned his mouth sour.

"We do what we can, learn more with each turn of the moon," Blakely expounded. "But still, 'tis not safe for females alone at night. Continue to keep yours inside and escorted at all times."

Not long after Luce crashed into his shop, enchanting both Brier and Barnabas with her verve and passion, Blakely had first rapped on the back door, advising Brier of nefarious happenings nearby and the need to watch over their women. Keeping the source of the warnings to himself, Brier nevertheless made sure his fellow shopkeepers—especially Hurwell, the horse-obsessed lout—knew to guard their womenfolk's safety.

Blakely had an uncanny ability to knock only when Brier would hear him, Luce washing her hair or sleeping upstairs any time the marquis sought a private word. So today was an aberration—seeing Blakely in sunshine, and not late at night.

As though the question showed on his face, Blakely pointed to the carriage he'd left with his coachman and tiger at the end of the alley. "We travel to our country homes for winter," he explained. "I have others in place to continue my work here, but Lady Blakely tells me I will be dawdling son or daughter upon my knee"—a least likely dawdler Brier couldn't fathom—"by spring, so... So away I take her."

For once, the man looked disconcerted, almost troubled by the notion of adding the cloak of fatherhood to his already burdened shoulders. But then Blakely banished any hint of uncertainty, resumed his stoic, unreadable expression and pulled a folded note from his pocket. "Here are my directions: in town, my club"—his *club*?—"and at my estate. I invite you to write—upon any topic." His lips tilted in what might be termed a half smile. "Does not always need be danger alone that is discussed between us."

Pleased by the invitation, Brier secured the note. "Thank you. I will. And I appreciate you stopping by."

"The Bug Man!" Lord Hammond surprised them both. "Clay? Your younger brother, yes? I believe he was a couple years behind me at academy."

"Before you were expelled?" Blakely asked, as only a disapproving older brother could.

"Prefer to think of it as being *rusticated*, myself." Lord Hammond flashed teeth and crinkled eyes, not intimidated—or ashamed—in the least. "Schoolage from those who know less of life than we? Pah. It mattered not, for as my favored bard would opine: *Yet he's gentle; never schooled and yet learned; full of noble device—*"

"Full of shat and not much sense," Blakely sniffed.

"*Noble* shat," Lord Hammond chortled.

Brier chuckled, enjoying the brotherly banter, comforted to realize he was pleased for Lord Blakely, at the idea of his family expanding, and not envious, not immediately downtrodden at the reminder of the cherished ones he'd grieved so long ago. As though time with Luce continued to heal the past as well as enhance his present.

"And now, we had best collect our females," Hammond added, with an indulgent chuckle. "Before they decimate your selection with their shopping."

The two headed back to their carriage, but not before Blakely said to Brier, "Continue to keep my presence here between us? While still sharing cautions where you can?"

"Always do I guard your privacy," Brier said truthfully, knowing now that Lord Blakely did indeed oversee a *sex club* and filing that little tidbit away—but not to bandy about. "For I know how difficult it can be to come by."

———⟶∘⟵———

"THERE NOW, Sir William, I do believe that looks right smashing."

Lucinda finished adjusting one of the silk embroidered shawls Thorne had sent with his last shipment from India. He'd included twenty of the beauties for Brier to price and sell—and four more, one for each of the women in his life: sisters Rose and Eve; mother, Evangeline; and sister-in-law, Luce.

Evangeline and Edgar, the first names of Brier's parents, she'd learned upon their visit early this year. (Hence the family's fascination with E names.)

Luce's shawl was tucked away upstairs, the peaceful blue—that Brier said reminded him of her eyes—folded lovingly around the snuff tin and Bible of her parents' and her grandmother's handkerchief, the cherished items mysteriously returned shortly after she and Brier met right before Christmas last.

Unlike the recent rains, this particular bright autumn day had burst upon London like a gift, the air crisp, the sun shining. Satisfaction in work well-done infused her being. Though long days on her feet, often bending or reaching, made muscles noticeably sore (much more so than sitting silently adjacent to a fractious pinch-penny) enjoying her evening meals with pleasant conversation—and a few demanding *merrows*—followed by snugging into bed alongside her husband was the stuff of dreams realized. Of yearnings fulfilled.

Her *husband*, a word she never tired of thinking or saying, who pulled her into his arms every chance he could.

Every time she took a moment to think of her bounty, her heart brimmed so full, Luce knew not how her stays still fit against her chest.

Her fingers fluttered over the shawl's rich scarlet background, made even more brilliant by the array of gold and colorful threads sewn over the surface. Against the polished metal, the rum shawl was sure to draw the attention of everyone who walked in. Brighter and bolder than what one usually found in England, even those they had received previously thanks to Thorne's travels.

Luce stared at Will's hard head. Ran her finger over the slightly askew "nose" and patted his breastplate. "You need a bonnet."

She cast about for just the right thing to complement their otherwise imposing newest addition, trying first one bonnet from a nearby selection, and then two more. "Neither of these will do either."

She frowned, knuckles folded beneath her chin as she surveyed her other choices.

The bell over the door announced customers, so she left the last one in place, quickly returned the other two and turned to welcome the pair entering the shop.

The slender blonde with the regal bearing and open smile—that gave no hint of her station —greeted Luce warmly. "Mrs. Chapman, your note came at the most fortuitous of weeks. For we are traveling from London today and I convinced my husband to let us stroll about a bit..." The young yet poised Lady Blakely gestured to the lovely female at her side. "Have you met my sister-in-law?"

Even younger, but with the most lush of figures—apparent despite the demure attire— and the blackest hair Luce had ever seen. But it was the headgear atop the raven strands that snared her.

Luce bustled closer with haste. "Your bonnet!" she exclaimed, forgetting to moderate her excitement as a shopkeeper no doubt should. "'Tis the most..."

Beautiful seemed inept. *Pretty*, insipid. How did one describe the most marvelous of masterpieces?

For balanced upon her head was a veritable spring garden. The blooms, leaves and vines woven throughout graced the piece with such texture and heart, Luce could practically smell the flowers from here, their scent wafting closer with every breath. Her fingers tingled to explore.

"Abominable?" The woman offered with a light toss of her head that only gave Luce a better look at the side. "Utter riddings? Rubbish?"

Luce gasped. "To call that creation garbage? How can you say such..."

The majestic-bonnet wearer only laughed, reaching up to take out the hat pins that kept the abundant confection anchored to her raven hair.

Luce's eyes widened to take in every speck. Speaking of abominable, the tingle in her fingers turned into an itch. She *needed* to touch. "How could you utter such blasphemy against this most stunning, most matchless of bonnets to ever grace CHAPMAN'S? London, even."

Ribbons danced and promenaded over the entire surface. Mostly pastels, save for a few hints of deeper, jeweled colors, in varying widths and textures. Some appeared curled and pinned. Some twined and sewn. Others spiraling in place or outward. A few narrow ones were braided... "It's as if a garden of delights swirls lovingly upon your head. Never have I seen headgear so glorious."

As she tugged the bonnet free of the last stubborn strand of hair, the younger woman's porcelain skin turned rosy. "Goin' to turn me over to the blush, you are."

She turned it topsy-turvy and handed it to Luce. The ordinary straw bonnet beneath the artistry was simple and sturdy, but when flipped over, when viewed from the sides and top...

Seeing the detailed work up close was like inspecting the shawls for the first time and marveling over the composition: the design someone had lovingly painted on with thread and talent. Only this with ribbons instead of silk.

Hoping she disguised her reluctance to relinquish it, Luce returned the bonnet to its owner. "Words fail me."

Lady Blakely chuckled. "I see I should have introduced my favorite sister-in-law—"

"Your *only* sister-in-law—"

"To my favorite shopkeeper. Mrs. Chapman, please meet Laney—erm, Lady Nash Hammond. Mrs. Chapman came to London recently and wed the proprietor."

"My feli...ci*tations*," her companion said, glancing at Lady Blakely, who nodded with a soft smile. "And call me Laney, please. *Lady Nash Hammond* is too uppish for me and *Eleanor* was another life ago, one I'd as soon forget, and *please*..." She leaned forward and whispered the rest. "Forgive my sometimes indelicate speech. My lips get sluggard when my *h*eart beats swift." A hint of uncertainty entered her expression. "You like my bonnet? Truly?"

"How can you doubt? 'Tis the most elegant, exquisite one I have ever beheld. Here or in Brighton."

"Lady Blakely." Brier entered from the back, carrying the heavy—and heavily wrapped—bundle tied with twine. "I readied your purchase the moment I heard your voice. A surprise, you said?" He indicated the package in his arms. "No one will see through this until you deign it's time."

"Perfect." Her gaze flicked from Brier's to Luce. "Did you peek? How do they look?"

"Impressive," said Brier, pride in his merchandise obvious. "Excellent craftsmanship. We found the right artist in Italy."

"Exquisite," Luce added, brushing her fingers over the paper as she had the lion statues themselves. "As with Laney's bonnet, whoever made these is talented indeed. They practically came alive in my hands."

Pleasure shone from Lady Blakely's expression. She placed one palm over her heart. "Thank you both. 'Tis a challenge to find the right gift for those who have every tangible thing they might want."

Lady Nash Hammond—Laney—snorted. "Or for those who would rather own naught at all."

The ladies shared a secret smile.

Beyond the bow window—empty of cantankerous cat, Barns curled upstairs by the hearth last she checked—a great traveling carriage rolled to a stop, crest on the black door.

"Ah, there they are now." Lady Blakely stood taller upon recognition.

"Have you a footman I can turn this over to?" Brier asked. "'Tis quite heavy."

A touch upon Luce's forearm drew her attention.

"May we talk? Over there?" Laney pointed at Will.

"Certainly."

Will. The suit of medieval armor—one of three—gifted to the family at the same time their great-great-grandfather was granted the title by the then king for some heroic act or other. Brier claimed no one in the family quite remembered how it all came about, the story being embellished during each telling. The "triplets" were separated and far from Yorkshire for the first time, gifted among the trio of oldest Chapman sons, Sharpe and Thorne doing who knew what with theirs.

But Brier? Spying the dismantled lot upon its unexpected arrival, he had sighed, then pulled out an engraved piece, tarnished but sturdy. "How do you feel about having a new display?" he'd asked with a devilish smile reminiscent of Thorne.

Nearing their new addition, Laney pointed to his hat. "I mean no ill intent, but *that* does not belong with *this*." She took an edge of the beautiful shawl and rubbed it lightly between two fingers. "If I may?"

Before Luce quite knew what the convivial female was about, she replaced the bonnet atop his helmet with her own. "There. Boundlessly better, aye?"

Luce grinned. "For him, yes. Not for you, though." She took the bonnet just removed from Will's helmet. "This one is infinitely less impressive than what you just shared."

Keeping her face averted from the others, Laney leaned toward Luce. "I made it. I can easily make another."

"You did not." The protest was instinctive, for ladies of the *ton* were not known for such pastimes.

Laney giggled. "I most certainly did. Was a milliner's assistant long ago. I adore making bonnets and you"—Laney gave her wrist a single squeeze—"*you* appreciate them. Unlike my Mr. Hammond who thinks they are that abomination I claimed earlier. That they are better left in a pigsty."

"Never say so! 'Tis a boon simply to behold."

"I shall make some for you," Laney declared. "And you shall keep what you wish and sell the others—"

"I couldn't." Couldn't imagine wearing such a fanciful bonnet herself. *Can you not?* some impish part of her normally sedate self prompted. *Can you not envision entertaining Brier, wearing a similar creation—and naught else?*

"Do not protest. Keep the knowledge that I made them to yourself, and when they sell?" Laney whispered beneath the sound of their bell, announcing others.

New voices, deeper ones, joined with the pair behind them.

"When they sell, please give the money to anyone in need. Anyone, anything—what or whomever you deem worthwhile will suffice."

Warmth like a blessing flowed over Lucinda. For she herself had been one in need such a short time ago. To be able to assist others? Even more than the small efforts she and Brier had begun? "Lady Na—" When the other woman shook her head, Lucinda acceded. "Laney, then. Henceforth, so it shall be. You honor me. With a weighty responsibility indeed."

Composed anew, Laney gave Luce a bright smile, satisfaction and pleasure both brimming from her. "One you are ideally suited for, I am sure."

With that mysterious statement echoing in Luce's mind, Laney rejoined the others. Leaving Luce in the dark—but still smiling.

Bonnets and bounties and the ability to aid others? Life had never been so grand.

———◦———

Yo, tomling. Bestir yourself.

Barnabas yawned. Tucked his head down and nuzzled the space between his furry little ears into the bed covers he had decided to grace with his worthy self not long ago.

Come now, we are to be off soon.

Another yawn. A slight twitch of one ear.

Do you not want to greet each other up close?

A hard twitch. Both ears, this time. "Mer?"

Right, man. Er, cat. Stir yourself and come down before we are off.

With one slumberous stretch, claws digging deep into the fabric, he roused sufficiently to jump down.

"Merrr-rrrr-rrrr!"

Aye, my next visit I shall send a pigeon ahead, to announce my arrival time—the chuckle came through as well—*you ornery creature.*

<hr>

AFTER RECORDING the purchases of three sisters who left in a noisy shuffle of parcels and people, Lucinda approached Brier where he still spoke with the two gentlemen: Lord Blakely and his brother, the elder now holding Lady Blakely's wrapped purchase.

Brier took her hand in his and pulled her into their circle. "Lord Blakely." Brier addressed the dark-countenanced lord with stiffly erect posture (who quite put her in mind of Thorne—with his regal bearing and untamed reputation). "May I present to you my wife? Mrs. Lucinda Chapman."

"Lady Chapman." Lord Blakely accompanied this with a gracious bow of his head.

So this peer knew who her husband was?

Interesting.

Lucinda couldn't stop the mental comparison to Brier's father, Edgar—for a more unusual, playful marquis she couldn't imagine. By contrast, from Lord Blakely's top hat down to the tips of his shining Hessians, everything immaculate in between, his was every bit the figure one would expect of a marquis: imposing, refined, body held erect and somewhat inflexible. His severe expression only softening when he glanced at his wife, who had stepped outside to visit with the sisters.

Lord Blakely's brother, Lord Nash Hammond, was anything but exceedingly stiff and proper. Similar to *his* wife—CHAPMAN'S new secret bonnet maker who Luce was delighted to work with—he exuded casual elegance, in both bearing and attire, while keeping himself slightly apart, as though he preferred avoiding the crush typically found in the city. Though he didn't speak as much as the others, giving her no opportunity to ascertain his personality, the lack of hat, carelessly tied neckcloth, and boots that had likely been shined—but not since last week—made her feel instantly at ease upon his quiet smile of welcome.

Just as she was finishing a curtsy in return—not overly obsequious, just respectful enough, she thought—toward Lord Blakely, Barnabas sailed into the room and bounded up onto the closest display, scattering merchandise with a clatter.

As the noise receded, half of them bent to retrieve items while the other half laughed. Placing what she collected on a nearby table, Lucinda turned to see Barnabas sitting directly in front of Lord Blakely, staring right at the roughly hewn man with nothing more than a slight sniff and swish of his tail.

"MEE-OWWW!"

Lord Blakely narrowed his eyes and gave the cat a tight smile.

"MerrRREOWLLLLL!"

The marquis inclined his head. *Bowing to their cat?* Lucinda had to bite her lips against the absurd chuckle that threatened.

To the overhead jingle, Lady Blakely came back inside in time to hear Barnabas start purring, the rumble as loud as thundering hooves.

"Well now"—Lady Blakely squeezed her husband's arm—"sounds as though you have made a new friend, my dark lord."

The feline gave a happy little hop before rising up on his back legs to knock the top of his head against Lord Blakely's chin.

Much like doting parents, Luce and Brier shared *a look*. Brier's half grin and raised eyebrows conveyed her surprise as well. *Who is this social stranger and what has he done with Barnabas?*

"It has been a sheer marvel, meeting you both." Wearing no bonnet at all, Laney gave Luce a hearty hug before pulling away to flash a happy grin. "I shall call—um, *shop*—again upon our return."

"I very much look forward to it."

Her husband's arm around her back, he nodded to everyone, then quietly took his leave, opening the door for her. "No demmed hat?" Luce heard him tell his wife. "I rather fancy this new look: *your hose ungartered, your bonnet unbanded, your dress unbuttoned, your...*"

Laney's laugh trilled behind them as the door closed.

"Mew."

Luce gave Barnabas a chin rub, to the accompaniment of more booming purrs. But instead of luxuriating in the attention he thought was his due, he whipped around to face Lord Blakely once again, head cocked, his ragged ear twitching.

Man and cat stared. Blinked once.

Barnabas turned his back on the marquis, flicked his tail against Blakely's jaw and hopped down, over to the window; empty of merchandise in the center, for they'd learned their lesson more than once.

Lady Blakely chuckled. "My, what was that all about?"

Her husband gave her an indulgent look, one that made his somewhat sinister features soften. "New friends, Francy."

He then turned his piercing gaze on first Brier

and then Lucinda. "New friends and the safety of others."

How was it he seemed bewilderingly familiar when she'd never met him before?

"Lady Chapman," he began, startling her with the seldom-used courtesy title that marrying the son of a marquis entitled her to, "I harbor great remorse that you arrived in London under particularly harrowing circumstances."

"Harrowing? Wh-why, *how* would you know?" She glanced toward Brier. "Did you...?"

A sharp shake of his head said *no*. A quick raise of his shoulders indicated *no idea*.

When she looked back at Lord Blakely, his expression remained inscrutable. "The cat told me."

From his dedicated spot in the window, Barns paused in his bath. "Merow. Mew. Rrrrowl!"

The marquis tipped his hat first to *the cat*, and then to them before he nodded toward his carriage beyond the window. "The horses grow restless, my dear."

"Aye, time to travel," Lady Blakely said. "Thank you again for finding what I requested. I will visit CHAPMAN'S again upon our return to London."

Lord Blakely opened the door for his wife, the heavy statues tucked under one arm as if they weighed no more than feathers.

Barnabas paused, stopped mid-lick to watch as Lord Blakely ordered a servant to secure the parcel and then handed his wife into the carriage.

"Mrrr?"

In the act of climbing in behind her, the marquis hesitated. Turned back and stared straight through their window.

"Mer? Rrrr!"

Then he was off, concealed inside the great carriage that rolled away and soon disappeared around the corner.

"Did he... Tell me he did not." Luce swallowed, a curious sort of wonder growing at the most peculiar last few moments. "He didn't. Did he?"

Brier came up behind her, slid one hand up her spine to her nape where his thumb rubbed a comforting caress. "By damn," he whispered, angling them both until they focused on where Barnabas had returned to his bath, "he *did*. The Marquis of Blakely just winked at our cat."

THE END

Thanks for reading!

I hope you had fun with Barnabas and his two humans. The moment I started writing, he tried to take over the show (as I'm sure you can tell). >^..^<

For more lighthearted holiday fun (with a dash of heat), check out my other Christmas Kisses, starting with Ed and Anne's story, *A Snowlit Christmas Kiss*.

Want to know what happens to Brier's neighbor, Mrs. Hurwell (a.k.a., Thea)? Her love is found a couple years later during 1815 in *Mistress in the Making,* a steamy, Regency-set historical. It's an emotional roller coaster of both angst and laughs featuring a lord burdened by a severe stammer.

Interested in the Roaring Rogues inhabiting London? Start with *Ensnared by Innocence*— Maggie Award of Excellence finalist—a super-steamy Regency-set Paranormal/Shifter novel featuring Lord Blakely (Luce's "beast") and one desperate lady who approaches the dissolute lord with a very inappropriate proposition…

To learn more about these books or any other good-ies, visit www.LarissaLyons.com.

ABOUT LARISSA

HUMOR. HEARTFELT EMOTION. & HUNKS.

A lifelong Texan, Larissa writes steamy regencies, blending heartfelt emotion with doses of laugh-out-loud humor. Her heroes are strong men with a weakness for the right woman.

Avoiding housework one word at a time (thanks in part to her super-helpful herd of cats >^..^<), Larissa adores brownies, James Bond, and her husband. She's been a clown, a tax analyst, and a pig castrator(!) but nothing satisfies quite like seeing the entertaining voices in her head come to life on the page.

Writing around some health challenges and computer limitations, it's a while between releases, but stick with her...she's working on the next one.

Learn more at LarissaLyons.com.

a amazon.com/author/larissalyons
BB bookbub.com/authors/larissa-lyons
g goodreads.com/larissalyons
f facebook.com/AuthorLarissaLyons
O instagram.com/larissa_lyons_author

LARISSA'S COMPLETE BOOKLIST

Historicals by Larissa Lyons

ROARING ROGUES REGENCY SHIFTERS

Ensnared by Innocence

Deceived by Desire

Tamed by Temptation (TBA)

REGENCY CHRISTMAS KISSES

A Snowlit Christmas Kiss

A Frosty Christmas Kiss*

A Moonlit Christmas Kiss (Dec. 2023)

*(expanded version of *Miss Isabella Thaws a Frosty Lord*)

MORE REGENCY CHRISTMAS KISSES

Rescued by a Christmas Kiss

MISTRESS IN THE MAKING series (Complete)

Seductive Silence

Lusty Letters

Daring Declarations

Mistress in the Making - Bundle

FUN & SEXY REGENCY ROMANCE

Lady Scandal

Lady Imposter (early 2024)

———◆———

Contemporaries by Larissa Lynx

SEXY CONTEMPORARY ROMANCE

Renegade Kisses

Starlight Seduction

SHORT 'N' SUPER STEAMY

A Heart for Adam...& Rick!

Braving Donovan's

No Guts, No 'Gasms

POWER PLAYERS HOCKEY series

My Two-Stud Stand*

Her Three Studs*

The Stud Takes a Stand (TBA)

*Her Hockey Studs - print version